LETTING GO

LETTING GO
Abe Aamidor

THE PERMANENT PRESS
Sag Harbor, NY 11963

For information, address:
  The Permanent Press
  4170 Noyac Road
  Sag Harbor, NY 11963
  www.thepermanentpress.com

Library of Congress Cataloging-in-Publication Data

Aamidor, Abraham author.
   Letting go / Abe Aamidor.
   Sag Harbor, NY: The Permanent Press, 2018.
   ISBN: 978-1-57962-538-2
      1. Middle-aged men—Fiction. 2. Fathers and sons—Fiction.
   3. Bereavement—Fiction.

PS3601.A217 L37 2018
813'.6—dc23   2018008969

Printed in the United States of America

To David and all the young soldiers who've stepped up.

CHAPTER 1

The Chilcot Report on the 2003 Iraq invasion and war was published today.

Mistakes were made. The UK should never have invaded. The UK could not trust American intelligence. The UK could not trust its own intelligence agencies.

"If we only knew then what we know now we would not have supported the war," the *Guardian* newspaper quoted a veteran Labour Party member as saying.

"But there's nothing new in the report," said a current Labour activist. "Everything that's known now was known then." Labour Party leader Jeremy Corbyn said he was too busy to read the report as he was visiting families of dead soldiers at the time it came out.

I close my laptop, I look out my rear window at a towering cottonwood tree as it releases its seasonal fluff, and I sigh my thousandth sigh. "Let Jeremy Corbyn come to Indianapolis and console me."

My son, Bertrand, is a fallen soldier, Afghanistan in his case. My wife, Thetis, who died a few years after Bertrand, would go to Crown Hill Cemetery, its glacial till originally dedicated to Union soldiers who fell in the Civil War, and she'd stand under an Alice blue sky in summer, the air warm

as a mother's breath itself, and recall moments from their
lives together as Madonna and child, maybe share news of
current events, basically just talk to him as if, well, as if.

We'd named our son after Bertrand Russell, the famous
philosopher who'd written *Why I Am Not a Christian* and the
antiwar essay, "Has Man a Future?" I'd studied him in college, yet it seems odd in retrospect—Russell the pacifist, the
man who would not be a Christian—but there we were
assembled, a Christian burial for our warrior son's human
remains. A small group of mourners stood under a simple
canopy tent—a friend of mine from work, a soldier who had
known Bertrand years earlier, and fellow nurses who worked
with Thetis at Saint Vincent Hospital. Thetis wanted to
speak first.

"Thank you all for coming," she began. "It's wonderful
to have friends who want to help but the truth is you can't.
So many times I tried to comfort parents who lost children in
the wards, tell them to be strong, say it's not ours to reason
why and some such, yet every time I secretly wondered,
'What if it were me? When would my knees buckle?' Now
I know."

The minister spoke next, predictably lamenting that a
young man had been deprived of life too soon and yet he
affirmed that we need not worry because Bertrand's immortal soul is in a better place now. "For if we believe that Jesus
died and rose again, even so them who also sleep in Jesus will
God bring with him."

When my turn to speak came I was unredeemed, citing
Russell chapter and verse as to why he was not a Christian—
it was because there is no evidence for God's truth, wish
fulfillment being merely an indication of our own existential
loneliness, and there is no evidence for the immortal soul,

either, hence that thing, too, is chimeric. But I also quoted from Alfred North Whitehead, a friend of Russell's.

"Your life matters because you did live it," he'd once said of any who perish. That I also believe.

CHAPTER 2

I finished a book the other day, *In Times of Fading Light*. It's by Eugen Ruge, whom I'd never heard of before, but it's a post-Cold War saga set in the former East Germany after its collapse. There's the patriarch, a respected theoretician and writer; the son, loyal to a fault; the grandson who comes to doubt; and the great-grandson who wants to tell the world to get lost. I think Tolstoy may have been wrong when he wrote that all happy families are alike, but every unhappy family is unhappy in its own way. Ruge knows better—*all* families are both alike and not alike in every way. Let me tell you a little of my family drama beginning with Grandpa Drago. Grandpa came over from Serbia in 1910 and settled in Gary, Indiana, where he worked in the steel mills. I knew Drago pretty well in his later years and he'd tell me harrowing tales of his life in the plants. Apparently it could be a pretty good show in those clangy, harshly lit circuses, orange embers floating in front of your eyes, wafts of hot air smothering you like a desert hamsin, and the men laughing ludicrously like brigands on a pirate ship as they did their high-wire act above big ladles of molten steel. "We didn't know anything about lung disease in those days," Grandpa told me once.

"During breaks we'd smoke Pall Malls and Lucky Strikes. Or just sit on the can for twenty minutes."

Grandpa looked the part, a man's man at six foot two, with dark, straight hair he cut short at the sides and combed straight back on top, and he had a toothy smile, all natural teeth too. I remember his eyebrows best—thick but not bushy, more like tree bark than tumbleweed. Grandpa served in World War I but wouldn't talk much about that part of his life. We knew he'd volunteered in 1917, then went straight to France where he served in an engineering unit, but they had to fight too. Grandpa said he liked Paris, the usual landmarks and all—once he talked about the dancers and then winked at Dad—but he wouldn't talk about the battles. When I was a boy I used to make toy rifles out of wood stripped from orange crates—the thicker pieces would be the stocks, then you'd nail two of the narrower side rails at an angle to make the barrels. Grandpa didn't like seeing those things, or me and the other kids lobbing water balloons at each other and making sounds with our mouths like explosions when real grenades would hit their mark. It's not that he said anything but I could always tell by the look on his face. We stopped those kinds of games after Grandpa grabbed a Roy Rogers cap gun from one of my friends and tossed it over the fence into a neighbor's yard.

Grandpa had married an Irish girl from the south side of Chicago, a former governess for an executive on the Illinois Central Railroad. She was real Irish, from some county in Ireland but I forget which. Unlike in the movies I don't think immigrants looked back all that fondly to the home country. Niamh took care of three children and everyone lived in a large manorial home on South Drexel Street with a carriage house in back before homes like that were subdivided into apartments. I've seen black-and-white "Kodaks" of the

home, as Grandpa always called snapshots, and they showed
two little girls in crinoline dresses and white stockings up to
their shins, tightly curled hair on top like Shirley Temple, and
the boy was just like Buster Brown, a suit with short pants
and a kind of bow tie around his neck, but not fully tied,
and highly polished shoes, of course. Grandpa said they'd
met at the Indiana Dunes when Niamh and the three kids
were swimming there; they'd taken the South Shore train
in and Grandpa had had the day off. I've seen a Kodak of
Grandma from that era in her bathing suit, probably navy
blue with white trim all around, including a square collar
down her back just like a real navy uniform, and the shorts
came down to her knees, a look that was dated even by the
time the photo was taken. You can just make out the Chicago
skyline at the far edge of the lake in the background and the
Gary smokestacks off to the left. Niamh is shyly toying with
her hair as the photographer snaps the picture and her smile
is more of a *You're not really going to make me do this, are you?* kind
of look, but she must not have resisted too strenuously.

Grandma died in 1930, died young, so I never knew her
and Grandpa never remarried. But he'd visit us in Indianapolis where Dad had settled after World War II. We'd all
sit around the kitchen table, a round oak pedestal table like
the farmers always liked, and they'd pour beer out of big
glass jug refills and maybe let me sniff but never drink it, and
Grandpa smoked quite a bit, too, so we kept the windows
open even in winter if that's when he was visiting, or he'd
just sit on the porch if it was summer and watch me and
the other kids in the neighborhood play. It was Grandpa's
death that has stuck with me the most from my childhood.
He'd come to live with us, not just visit, in the last year of
his life. He was alone and getting old and Dad wouldn't
abide that, so we drove up to Gary one day to fetch him

and his things. It was two-lane blacktop all the way as I-65 hadn't been completed yet and we passed by tall cornfields, cylindrical concrete silos, barbed wire cow pastures, and old barns with weathered wood planks and cat slide roofs, lots of roadside vegetable stands, too, and it took four hours up and four hours back but we did it all in one day, the packing included. "Are you sad to leave home?" I asked Grandpa. "Do you want to sit in the front? We got a whole room set up for you nice, Grandpa." He hobbled into the car, Dad gripping him by the shoulders, and Grandpa looked like a bird, his skin thin like dragonfly wings, and he just said how nice it was of us to come and get him, that he'd never want to be any bother. We drove through some small towns I'd heard about in school so I must have been at least in fourth grade by then because that's when you study local history in Indiana. We passed near Valparaiso, which was where the Bears always had their training camps. When I asked Dad if we could swing by their practice field even if they weren't there then, just to see it, and I asked Grandpa if he wanted to see it, too, Dad looked at me in the rearview mirror and smiled so I knew the answer was no. Later we drove past Peru where the circus always wintered, which I thought was funny because you leave Indiana in the winter if you can, not come here, and Dad just said, "Next time," without turning to look at me. Grandpa was becoming restless in his seat and Dad asked if he needed to go pee and he said he did and Dad asked if I needed to go pee, which I didn't, but when we pulled up to a roadside stand with an outhouse in back Dad said I should go with Grandpa and help him, and then I should try to pee. After we rolled to a stop on the gravel I ran out of the car and opened the passenger door for Grandpa and I saw that he wasn't sitting up so straight but was slouching and his left shoulder seemed curled, even twisted, and none of his clothes fit, not the blue jeans and not the wool waist jacket, and I helped him by his arm like I was a crutch and we shuffled over to the outhouse. "I'll be all right," he said when we got to the door and I told him I'd just wait outside. But when he opened the door, he said something like, "Ooh, wee," and he held his nose and then turned to me and we both laughed.

Back in the car Dad and Grandpa talked a little about the coal miners' strike in West Virginia that year and Grandpa kept muttering, "Dyin' industry. Dyin' industry, all of it," but didn't comment further about it. We drove on and the car bobbed up and down on the uneven roads and I felt motion sickness come on. Dad noticed but I wouldn't let him stop the car just for me and I concentrated hard so I wouldn't throw up. Grandpa asked if I wanted the front seat—watching the horizon always helps, he said—so Dad stopped the car and we changed seats. Once on our way again I thought to ask Grandpa if he wanted to know how I was doing in school, which was a trick all kids use when they want to tell you something but don't want to appear pushy. He told me that would be fine and I told him about a math quiz where I got a perfect score and that I might go out for the baseball team when I got into middle school and even about this girl I talked to a lot, how we always walked part of the way home together before she had to turn off onto a different street. I had a lot to talk about and I just kept talking but then I noticed that Grandpa had fallen asleep, that he was now lying across the bench seat. Dad turned to me then. "You can tell him everything later, Dwight," he said. "I'm sure he'll want to hear all about school when we get home."

We'd set up a nice room for Grandpa and we'd leave the window shade up for him at night, so he could see the full moon that loomed large through the trees especially in the fall when it would rise just after dark and the leaves had been thinned pretty well. Once I saw Grandpa looking so intently at the stars which still shimmered clearly over Indianapolis in the 1950s. "What do you see?" I asked him.

"I see you being born," he said to me that time. I didn't understand him then but I do now.

Grandpa would let me sit on the edge of his bed and look out the window with him if I wanted and sometimes I'd read from a book report I'd done or just read a Red Smith sports column aloud and I remember the cracks Smith made about "whistle ball" because the refs were calling so many fouls during basketball games. I had to turn my shoulder toward Grandpa a little when I'd read but it wasn't too awkward, not at all.

I was with Grandpa when he died. We'd gone outside to sit on the porch and watch the cars go by, hear the kids play on the streets, "Hello, Mr. Bogdanovic," some of them said and he just waved back. The day he died I was talking to him about another girl in class who liked me, or maybe she was just fussing over my hair because she liked my hair and I thought it was funny that a girl would do that. It was a crisp autumn day, Halloween just over, and the dry leaves in the yard spiraled in little dust devils, and I turned around to ask Grandpa, "What do you think of a girl who would do that?" and he was slumped over in the rocker we'd bought for him, bought just so he could sit on the porch and watch the world go by and I have to say that I realized immediately what had happened and no one had to tell me to be strong, I had been preparing for this moment like spring training for Little League and so I was strong. Dad was home at the time fixing dinner, so it must have been a Thursday afternoon when Mom worked late, and he was frying lake trout in a pan and cooking wild rice in a copper pot, I think, and

I went into the kitchen and looked up at him, maybe my lips
quivered, and he looked at me as knowingly as I looked at
him, and he took my hand and we both walked out calmly
to the porch.

WE HAD a small house on Sherman Drive for a few years,
right near a large park and greenhouse, but the neighborhood never caught on with the yuppies like some others did,
that is, after all the good blue-collar jobs disappeared, disappeared like the bee hives in the wealds. Still I had a lot of
friends and all of us kids were free to ride our bikes anywhere and play outside and if child predators existed they
must have dreamed of molesting young boys while locked
in their bathrooms fondling themselves because I never
heard of a boy or girl actually being assaulted. Kids could
earn money delivering the newspaper every morning before
school or selling Christmas cards every autumn for the Junior
Sales Club of America—get fifty cents back on each box
sold or earn points toward a new English three-speed racer
or other prizes. We raked leaves in the fall, shoveled snow
in winter, and carried grocery bags home for housewives on
Friday afternoons—women would give you a quarter for that
but sometimes you just helped because it was the right thing
to do. I know the 1950s weren't really *that* ideal, not if you
were black or a migrant farmworker or even an Okie from
Muskogee, I know that *now*, but there was a lot that was right
in that decade. At least, it was good to me.

I remember my mother resting on her patented four-
way Contour Comfort Chair after a hard day selling fashions at the L. S. Ayres department store downtown, which
was her part-time job when I was younger. When she'd get
home after working late on Thursday evenings or all day

on Saturdays she would carefully put away her uniform-like low heels, starched white shirt, and dark skirt in a closet, then don a terry housecoat. She did watch *Queen for a Day* on TV on her days off and she'd sometimes talk about the lady who'd won a new refrigerator or just a sewing machine and she admitted that she'd like to win something like that, but would it look like begging if she were to go on one of those shows? Mom would never beg for anything; no one in our family would ever do that. For my confirmation I got a nice pair of trousers, a high-thread-count dress shirt, and a real silk tie, all from L. S. Ayres, and Mom said she would have bought me these nice things even without her employee discount. We had a good laugh and, at the time, I didn't have any problems with being confirmed. Well, you know what's coming—she died when I was in high school, developed ovarian cancer or uterine cancer, what does it matter, it was virulent, and when they kept her in the hospital to await death they wouldn't let me see her, so I guess not everything in the old days was done right. I was cheated out of my last moments with my mother but more than that she was cheated—after all it was her life.

Dad's turn at war came with Hitler and Stalin, Churchill and Roosevelt. He went up to Toronto in 1940 and volunteered for the Canadian Army. I don't know if it was because he hated the Fascists so much—Grandpa certainly did because the Fascists had occupied and carved up Serbia pretty good—or maybe he knew it was just a matter of time before the United States would become involved in the war anyway. Yet Dad never spoke about his war any more than Grandpa did ("You don't want me to give you a lecture, do you?" he once said in anger, really snapped at me) but his tour of duty ended with Operation Market Garden. He was

a paratrooper with the British RAF by then and he was shot
up bad, which is poor English, but that's how Mom always
put it—"shot up bad," or "shot up real bad." I read a little
about the operation when I was in high school and they
made a movie about it too. Market Garden was the plan
in 1944 to drop behind German lines and clear the way for
an Allied advance across the Rhine River but there was one
bridge they couldn't capture, which was the "bridge too far."
A lot of people use that as a metaphor now but I wonder
how many know where it comes from.

"Your father would talk to his fallen comrades at night
when he came home from the war," Mom told me once. "It
was like they were still making jokes or exchanging pictures
of their girlfriends or maybe complaining about the rations.
You'd think it was all good times but it wasn't. He never cried
but I would."

I used to think of bravery like the Medal of Honor winners I'd read about, men who'd throw themselves into the
line of fire, either to rescue an injured comrade or to foil an
enemy advance, all without regard to their own safety. *"Without regard to their own safety,"* which is part of the criteria for
being awarded the medal. Yet my father had saved a newspaper clipping from World War II, "The Death of Captain
Waskow," written by Ernie Pyle, a native Hoosier.

> "At the front lines in Italy, Jan. 10, 1944–
> "In this war I have known a lot of officers who were
> loved and respected by the soldiers under them. But never
> have I crossed the trail of any man as beloved as Capt.
> Henry T. Waskow of Belton, Texas.
> "Capt. Waskow was a company commander in the 36th
> Division. He had led his company since long before it left
> the States. He was very young, only in his middle twenties,
> but he carried in him a sincerity and gentleness that made
> people want to be guided by him . . . .

"I was at the foot of the mule train the night they
brought Capt. Waskow's body down . . . . Dead men had
been coming down the mountain all evening, lashed onto
the backs of mules. They came lying belly-down across the
wooden pack-saddles, their heads hanging down on the left
side of the mule, their stiffened legs sticking out awkwardly
from the other side, bobbing up and down as the mule
walked . . . ."

I didn't find the clipping until years after Dad died; by
then I already was old enough to know why he never wanted
to talk about war and the Ernie Pyle column was merely
confirmation, not revelation, except that I felt the pain Dad
had felt even more keenly because of it. I think the column
also helped me understand why I'd been named after General Eisenhower; Dad was ambivalent, as was Eisenhower
himself.

Dad settled in Central Indiana because he'd gotten a job
in Beech Grove repairing railroad cars; it's near the south
side of Indianapolis so that's why he settled there. Pay was
decent too. I'd always ask Dad what his day was like when
he'd come home and he'd say he almost lost a hand to a
circular saw or a toe when someone dropped an anvil, then
he'd smile and tousle my hair and ask about my day. I think
most kids growing up think their fathers must be like all other
fathers and vice versa, which is how I figured it was too.
Well, there were drunks and wife beaters and suicides, I'm
sure, but most fathers I knew really were alike—dependable,
hard-working, somewhat stoic, and modest in their tastes. No
one I knew owned a Cadillac or Lincoln and we didn't even
know what a Volvo was.

Dad wasn't much of a churchgoer, unlike Mom had been.
I don't think that's where I got my skepticism though. Most
of my friends and their families certainly attended church,
and Catholic, Protestants, and Orthodox all got along. We'd

read the *Studs Lonigan* trilogy in high school and while I liked the kids in those stories because they were a lot like me I couldn't understand the religious antagonisms. I guess that was one good thing that came out of World War II.

Then, one day, like the old lyric, "Turn around, turn around," it was I who was the father. I still have in my garage one of those large galvanized steel washtubs that Thetis would set out on the back porch when she'd do the laundry, that is, before we bought a Kenmore washer and dryer from Sears. I repurposed it as a pet turtle habitat filled with rocks and twigs after a friend brought me a tiny turtle he'd won at the Marion County Fair. Bertrand was seven or eight at the time and I wanted to make him happy. "Look close," I told him. "There's his head. There's the wrinkled skin on his neck. You're Godzilla and he's the human."

Bertrand had just lost his dog, Spot, a beagle mutt and not very creatively named, I suppose. Bertrand loved the dog but it ran away one day.

"Did you leave the backyard gate open?" I asked him at the time. Bertrand shook his head and didn't look up, and he said he hadn't left the gate open.

"Are you sure?" I pressed, but Thetis told me to leave the boy alone, that he was sad enough and he had to grieve in his own way.

Bertrand later came to me in a dark corner of the night and said he had, in fact, left the gate open. "I don't ever want to lie again," he said, and then we hugged and had a good cry together.

The turtle was a hit, but they can live for forty or fifty years which concerned me because that's a long time to hold a little boy's interest. Nonetheless Bertrand would diligently chop carrots and beets into fine pieces to feed the turtle and change out the water, too, but this one only survived a few

months. I asked Bertrand if he wanted to bury the little crea-
ture and he said he would, that he had to be the one to do it.

During one summer vacation, I invented something I called
Dad's Funner Summer Camp. I would take Bertrand to the
nearest ball diamond and teach him baseball—he was a little
older by then and what was I waiting for! The diamond was
about two miles from home so we could bike there, which
is what we did. Bertrand already rode on twenty-four-inch
wheels and I had a Schwinn at the time, though it was really
a rebranded Taiwanese import by then, and every day he'd
want to race me to the park and I'd say it's too dangerous,
watch out for traffic, and all that, and of course we'd race
to the park anyway.

"I know you're gonna catch me," he'd shout when we
neared the diamond.

"You wouldn't want me to let you win, would you?" I'd
shout back, then I'd overtake him. I thought it built character.

We had the baseball diamond to ourselves most mornings during Funner Summer Camp. I can still see Bertrand
crouched at the shortstop position, knees bent, he's pound-
ing his leather glove and wiping his nose with the back of
his hand as I begin hitting grounders to him. The first day I
hit some weak grounders to Bertrand on purpose, then I hit
them harder and a little wider to the right and to the left.
Sometimes I'd fake him out by looking in one direction and
hitting the other way; that always made him laugh and that
made me smile.

He made good progress, but I may have pushed him too
hard because he discovered soccer at the YMCA that fall. I
was glad he discovered something; that's all I really wanted.
Sound body and mind—yes, I believed in the "Y" motto.
Bertrand liked his little uniform, which for some reason
had the same colors as the Carolina Panthers football team,

especially that bluey slate aquamarine color even though his "Y" team was sponsored by a hardware chain famous for the color red. Bertrand hemmed and hawed when we wanted to take a series of photos of him at practice one afternoon that fall but I think he loved it. "You can watch me play, Dad," he'd say. "Just don't talk to me when I'm with the other guys." Maybe he was nine or even ten when he said that. It's at about that age when kids start asserting their independence. I didn't mind. I always knew that parenting is the one job where the goal is to put yourself out of business.

When he was a little older I took him to the Old Hoosier Amusement Park, a crappy little attraction near out-of-the-way Thorntown. All the rides had been purchased second-hand from traveling carnivals and defunct kiddielands, things like small roller coaster rides on assemble-it-yourself steel rails and water slides not much taller than a two-story build-ing, even shaggy Shetland ponies that were tied by long poles to a central wheel. The state had been trying to close the place for years but the park was popular with working class families because admission was cheap and everyone else who went there looked pretty much like you did. They sold ham-burgers on white bread buns from a gas-fired grill along with house brand soda pop they'd purchased in bulk from Kroger, but Thetis had packed peanut butter sandwiches, bananas, and homemade lemonade in a single thermos for us. It was cheaper and it was healthier. More than that, it was enough.

Bertrand's favorite ride was the Tilt-a-Whirl, which was little more than a collection of tin buckets you, and up to three other souls, could sit in that were connected by steel cables to a spindle in the center. The faster the spindle turned, the higher the rides went due to centrifugal force. None of that was exceptional. It was the rudders. The Tilt-a-Whirl featured steerable rudders that looked like they came from

Stearman biplanes that had been scrapped and they allowed you to dip and climb and flutter like a bug in a strong wind.

We even tried the water slide that day. Some kids went up the ladder in their street clothes while others, especially younger boys, simply stripped down to their underwear. One lady in a tank top and shorts took her dog with her and no one objected though a few people pointed fingers or stared. Bertrand and I had not come prepared for this but he suggested we go up in our clothing, too, and I always wanted to please him if I could, not merely give him things, and unless I had a valid objection I wouldn't say no. We set our shoes aside and went up and down the slide several times, hurrying to get back in line after each trip, and the only mishap was when my sunglasses came off. We tried to spot them in the pool at the bottom of the attraction and Bertrand even jumped back in from the sides but with the constant agitation from people hitting the pool and the fact that the water wasn't too clear to begin with there wasn't much chance of success. Plus, they kicked us out of the park. Maybe they thought Bertrand was diving for loose change.

We never took big vacations—no Disney World, no Washington Monument, or Lincoln Memorial—but we went on plenty of smaller ones close by in the Midwest and always integral to nature. There was the time we rented a cabin at Pokagon State Park near Angola; it was the refrigerated toboggan run that drew us there. We bought Bertrand a one-piece snowsuit, insulated boots, and thick mittens at a Farm and Fleet because Thetis thought the temperature might be too cold and I asked her if the Civilian Conservation Corps boys who'd built the toboggan run during the Great Depression would have said the same thing. Thetis thought she would stay in and knit or read, I forget which, but Bertrand yanked on her arm and helped her don her own boots and long wool coat. The rented toboggans were traditional wood slats bound together in parallel with a curved nose in front, what everyone has seen in old Christmas movies or at least in an L.L. Bean catalog. Bertrand wanted to sit at the front and I told Thetis to sit in the middle and hold him by the waist, then I'd jump in back and hold on to her. But when our turn came I was slow in getting into position and the toboggan started down without me. "Hold on, you can do it, Thetis," I cried from behind.

"Hold on, you can do it, Bertrand," I heard her cry as the toboggan sped ahead.

After two hours going up and down I suggested we go into town and find a restaurant that served hearty stew and fresh baked bread and all agreed.

Bertrand enjoyed school. I think it was because he could turn every homework assignment into a game. Not just how many questions he could get right, then better the score next time, which he also did, but it was that after he'd learned to use an abacus he would solve all his arithmetic problems on one, or if he was studying history he'd speculate on how the world might be different if Davy Crockett was a Chickasaw Indian or Casimir Pulaski had been appointed commander-in-chief of the Continental Army, not George Washington, oddball alternate universes like that. He could play these games for hours.

In his freshman year in high school, Bertrand was recruited to sort out the free lending library the nurses at Saint Vincent's ran for patients. It was just one former break room with a couple of hundred books but they had no inventory tracking system so I suggested that Bertrand might make up a card catalog for a school project. Thetis thought it was a stellar idea and said it would be wonderful to see Bertrand every afternoon for a week or two while he completed the project. Bertrand was very diligent. He created a Dewey Decimal number for each title and both a subject and author index in a metal card file; the staff even presented him with a Parker pen and pencil set when he was finished as a reward.

Bertrand proved to be a proper teenager, respectful of his elders, kind to strangers, and chivalrous with young ladies. I remember his first date—he asked Thetis and me if it would be all right to invite a certain girl to dinner and a show. He was fourteen at the time.

"And who is the young lady?" Thetis asked. She and I were seated on our living room sofa; Bertrand had announced that he had something to tell us and he requested that we be seated first. He stood in front of us as if he were making a presentation.

"She's in two of my classes," he said. "She's very smart. We're lab partners in biology. We were assigned to each other by the teacher. When it came time to cut up a frog she asked if she could do it and I said, 'Please!' She laughed so hard it was, like, it was infectious, and I knew right away that she was someone I could like."

I remember the dialogue perfectly. He didn't say that he liked her immediately, but that he knew immediately she was someone he *could* like. He was so reflective, so incisive, so mature. At fourteen.

"She sounds wonderful," Thetis said. "We'd like to meet her." Thetis took my arm and patted it when she said that, her way of saying, "Wouldn't we, Dwight?"

Patricia—that was the girl's name—was quite a looker. Almost as tall as Bertrand, she was developing quite nicely, to use the now-obsolescent euphemism, but she dressed modestly, wore a full cotton dress the first time we met her, bodice all the way up to her neck, and her mahogany hair was pulled back and tied in a long ponytail. She curtsied when we greeted her at the door.

"Patricia figured she might as well call on me as you wanted to meet her anyway," Bertrand explained at the time. He said he'd already met her parents.

"So what's showing at the theater?" I asked.

"*Crouching Tiger, Hidden Dragon,*" Patricia quickly answered. "I think we all need to learn more about other people's cultures, including through the cinema."

"It's been out for a while. And it's not rated 'R,'" Bertrand added.

"Well, there'll be time for that," I said, and Thetis punched me with her elbow but it was OK as we all laughed, including Patricia.

A few months later, after a long study session with Patricia up in his bedroom and she'd already gone home, Bertrand came downstairs and said he wanted to speak with me. He looked at Thetis who was reading a magazine under a lamp and he didn't have to say anything, she understood that he wanted to speak to me alone. I put down my own book and sat upright a little, and asked Bertrand what was on his mind.

"Dad, when you were fourteen, did you have desires, you know, sexual desires? I don't want to be vague, but you know what I mean, don't you?"

I hesitated before answering. "Sure," I said. "We're an evolved species and we develop according to a schedule. Some people think it's a divine plan, but I think it's DNA." That brought a little smile to Bertrand's face.

"Well, first, I don't want you to think Patty and I have had sex or anything like that. Her parents would never allow it, for one thing, and she has too much respect for her own body to be, you know, loose."

I nodded.

"But, you see, I get so excited. You know what I mean."

I tried not to smirk; Bertrand might have taken it the wrong way. It was just that I couldn't help but think then that every man on Earth in the history of the world would know what he meant.

"Well, I was so excited, you know, and Patty could see it."

I interrupted him. "I think she's an extremely mature young woman," I said. "I'm really impressed by her. I don't know how to tell her that, but I'm impressed by the both of you. I want you to know that."

"Yeah, well, the thing is, Patty saw I was excited and she just slowly stuck her hand down there and I, well, I just creamed my pants so bad. I felt so ashamed but she said, 'It's all right. It's all right.' I never felt anything better in my life. I just let myself go."

I used to think I was a very progressive father, mostly because I was, but I was taken aback. Not because there was anything shocking there—the young have to discover and discover for themselves—but I was so struck by Bertrand's candor and forthrightness and especially his trust in me, which meant a lot.

"Well, you're not going to hell for anything like that, neither you or Patricia," I said. "But it's only going to get more challenging in the future, more tempting. You have to know when to stop."

"Not go too far, you mean."

Bertrand continued to look to me; a plea for guidance and approval was written all over his face. *Bertrand is almost a man*—that's what I suddenly realized then. And I was so eager to know who that man might be.

Overall, high school was a good experience for Bertrand. Lots of people remember cruel classmates, sitting alone in the lunchroom, or being ignored by a teacher who didn't think you had the stuff to excel, while the alternative kids and the "geeks and freaks" always felt marginalized. None of that applied to Bertrand. He made the soccer team, played midfield, maybe the team wasn't a competitor for the state championship but they won as many games as they lost, and he was active on the Human Relations Club, what these days would be called the Diversity Club. I didn't want to know this but the first girl he slept with was in the same club. It wasn't Patricia. How did I learn about it? Thetis found two unused prophylactics on the floor in Bertrand's room after the club had gone on a trip sponsored by the University of Kentucky to meet with students from more than thirty countries, I think that was the count, some sort of harmless "Kumbaya" event. Everybody had slept in tents in a nearby park in Lexington; there were chaperones but, you know, humans will be humans. We didn't want to confront Bertrand as such but we felt we had to initiate a conversation. We started by putting the unopened packages on the dining room table where we all were seated at the time. We'd set the dimmer on low which, with the lacy white tablecloth, almost made it seem like we were holding a séance.

"These come in three-packs, right?" I began.

Bertrand didn't look up at first. He just shrugged uncomfortably, then mumbled something like, "I guess so." I'd never been good at talking about sex to Bertrand, maybe because my dad never talked much to me about it, just a knowing jab in the chest if something risqué came on television or maybe there was a photo in the papers of Hugh Hefner in his silk robe with a buxom blonde bunny at his side. Or, maybe embarrassment over sex was generational—we *did* want boys to learn about it in the street; we *did* want boys to learn about it from "loose" women; we *did* want boys to learn about sex from drinking the water or some such nonsense.

Thetis took the lead as she'd previously said it was time after she'd found some cum stains on his sheet while doing the laundry one weekend. She said she'd buy a book, too, and when I squirmed or maybe said, "Oh, boy," but somewhat facetiously, she offered to buy two. But the talk she gave to him at the time must have done some good. After all, Bertrand used protection in Kentucky.

Bertrand explained that the girl had been making eyes at him for some time and he admitted he didn't necessarily like her that much. "She had to throw herself at me to get me," he said. "I didn't know I had any groupies."

We asked if the girl's parents knew and again Bertrand shrugged, then he wanted to know if we were going to call them. Thetis, always perfect in her timing, said she thought it best if we did. I asked Bertrand if he was going to see the girl again and he said he didn't want to but they both were still in the club and might be in the same classes in the future. He was a junior at the time.

"So you just used her for sex," I said. "You don't really like her but you saw you could have sex with her?"

It was only then that his lips started to quiver, he bent his head low, and then he began to softly weep.

CHAPTER 3

It's a Sunday afternoon and I receive an emergency callout from Matt at the Indianapolis Airport USO—another volunteer has canceled his shift and they need someone to fill in. I'm on a short list for emergency relief and my name came up next on the Rolodex, which Matt still uses. Matt is the volunteer coordinator. Gruff sounding like a drill sergeant, at least the ones we've all seen in the movies, he likes to threaten shutting down the center if he doesn't get someone to fill in, "And I mean fast!" Unlike most of the other volunteers, I'm not a veteran, but I tell myself that I don't want to be like all the corporate honchos, Washington insiders, and even ordinary citizens who always say, "I salute your service," then party on. It's for Bertrand too. What else can I do for him now?

I've volunteered for several years. I have the time, I meet interesting people, and I can eat all the Hot Pockets and canned Chef Boyardee meals I want, which is what we serve the young soldiers and their families in transit. It takes me about thirty-five minutes from my home in Carmel, a suburb immediately north of the city, to reach the airport. I have a well-kept 2004 Mustang GT, not really that fast and I don't drive it hard, either, but it's a convertible and I like to put the top down, a bit of a magic carpet ride for me down I-465, the ring road that surrounds Indianapolis. Businesses front the highway as in any city, insurance agencies, law firms, even a home oxygen supply company, all showcased in mid-rise buildings with prefab facades that will never be commemorated in any architectural history. I saw a banner strung from the outside wall of a nursing home the last time I made the trip, "Now accepting applications." It wasn't for hired help but *to get in, to live there.*

I tell Matt, sure, I'm available, and I ask what the problem is with Rupert, the guy who was supposed to be on duty. I'm not being nosy; it's just to be civil. Matt grumbles something and we move on.

The USO lounge is on the baggage-claim floor at the airport. The main room is about forty feet by seventy-five plus there's a small kitchen and separate, walk-in pantry that we keep secured. We have a big-screen TV, which is pretty standard these days, and lots of overstuffed chairs, plus two computers guests can use and even video games for the children, though lots of the younger soldiers while away their time with the games themselves. I try to make small talk with the soldiers when I can—"Where you coming from? Heading to? How long you been in?"—and sometimes they tell me and sometimes they don't. It's hard to compete with smartphones, I guess. Or video games. I'm told we had a lot of traffic during the big build-up in Iraq, but it's been relatively quiet the few years that I've volunteered, mostly people coming home from Afghanistan, where my son had been, or on their way to Camp Atterbury, which is about forty-five miles southeast of the airport. The camp is most notable for housing Italian prisoners of war during World War II and they have a small museum set up to commemorate those days complete with original cabins, bunk beds, and showers. They say the Italians didn't want to leave.

On this night it's very quiet as I have no guests for the first two hours. I watch a baseball game on TV and don't pay a lot of attention to the score but it's just that Bertrand and I used to watch games on Saturday afternoons together. He always loved the little animal iconography on the Orioles and Cardinals jerseys and even the halo on the Angels Disneyesque "A." After a bit I turn to CNN but all the news is too depressing, too urgent, or too distant, and next I switch to the movie channels but nothing piques my interest—either I've seen the film before, seen something like it, or I have to ask, "How do bad movies get made?" (Hint: They could get the financing.) There's a tape-delay auto race on the Speed Channel—I decide to watch that—and then I have to laugh at myself. Thetis would tease me each year that I went to the 500-Mile Race in Speedway. "They just go round and round, and at the end of the race one car wins and everyone else loses," she'd say, which was hard to argue with.

Finally, one guy steps up to the front counter, yet he's not signing in. He says he just wants to look the place over. We don't give tours as such but I don't want to be rude and I ask him if he's active duty or retired, which I hope is a subtle way of saying this is not the United Club; it's a lounge for military families only. He tells me he works over at FedEx in logistics and he just wanted to see the place. "I've worked at the airport for seven years and never stopped in, you know," he says. I don't invite him in, but I tell him what we do in twenty-five words or less and he makes a mental snapshot or two of the place in his head, then he drops a five-dollar bill into our collection jar and leaves.

Soon a young woman comes in—I say young but she's in her thirties and she seems very harried, even agitated—and I smile and say hello. She pulls out a Disabled American Veterans card, hard plastic, red, white, and blue, and she begins to sign her name on the register as if she's done this many times. "Do you have a military ID?" I ask and she looks up at me, startled, but doesn't speak at first. "You need a CAC card or other military ID to use the lounge, not something from a private nonprofit," I say. I'm not speaking in any kind of authoritarian voice. I'm not a police officer trying to establish control over the situation, but the woman erupts, she slams the pen on the counter, and jumps back.

"I've never had to show a military ID before," she claims, almost screams, and I'm not exaggerating either. I consult my cheat sheet with photos of all the acceptable forms of ID but I know that a Disabled American Veterans card isn't one of them. I look up at the woman again but say no more, which is another technique I've learned. I figure they've been told the rules before so I'm just trying to show that I'm enforcing them and usually they'll get the message and leave of their own volition. Maybe I've embarrassed the woman though. She charges off, not necessarily in a straight line, either, and I can tell that she's very upset, even more so than when she came in. I know there's a story behind her actions and I feel bad, and I decide to log everything and check with the volunteer coordinator later about what to do next time. Maybe a DAV card should be enough.

Next enters a young man in civvies. I see his hands first—he's presented me with his passport, which is unusual, then he smiles wanly and stuffs it back awkwardly in his front pants pocket and pulls out a Common Access Card—that's the CAC card. He's on the short side of average height, maybe five foot nine, and muscular enough but not like a body builder, not bulked up or thick-necked at all, just healthy looking like a good soccer or tennis player. I can't divulge his identity but I must describe him in some detail; you'll understand the reason soon enough. Let's just call him Stephen. Stephen has short, dark hair, not so much curled as eddied, and he's wearing a button-down, short-sleeved shirt, light blue, and dark trousers, cuffed, very preppy-looking except that everything is wrinkled. He is a soldier but I think he's traveling incognito, or has been.

"Where you coming from?" I ask in a very social way as he signs the register, but what I'm really thinking is that Stephen looks pretty fucked up. He's practically leaning on one elbow on the counter and he's got scum at the edges of his mouth. I figure he hasn't slept in a long time.

Stephen laughs through his nose, straightens up, and puts down the pen. "Oh, around," he answers, vague, mysterious. I notice that he has no luggage, not even a backpack or computer case. For a moment I think he's on the run but I know better. Well, he is on the run but he's not AWOL or anything like that. Elude is more like it. I ask where he's headed. He smiles at me but, again, doesn't answer. I tell him I'll make fresh coffee if he wants; there's some cheesecake in the fridge, I add. This soldier is too good for Hot Pockets and Chef Boyardee, I think. He plops down on one of the plush recliners, sighs, and spreads his legs. I try to see where his eyes are focused but I can't tell. I just know it's not anywhere here.

I step outside the lounge so I can study the Arrivals screen—Which plane just got in ten or fifteen minutes ago?—that's what I want to see. Recent arrivals are from Saint Louis, Orlando, and Toronto. Yep, that's probably the one. Toronto. He passed through there, covering his tracks, basically. Well, I know the story already. The kid's in special ops, maybe what they sometimes call grey ops, real Jason Bourne shit, but the real Jason Bourne, not some actor in a script that has to end well. Maybe he had to shake the hands of a warlord or pay off an opium dealer. Or maybe it was Iran-Contra all over again. I'm thinking rogue arms dealers who would be transferring American weapons to some insurgency while we get to maintain an arms-length relationship to the conflict. Or maybe he just had to kill someone, walk up to the vic from behind, come out of the dark with the silencer in place, or thrust a shiv into someone's liver and kidneys, then turn and run down the nearest alley. Yes, this shit really happens and it's kids like Stephen who pull it off, kids not much older than kids who stage frat house keggers or the hipsters in Brooklyn who walk around in Converse All Stars and secondhand varsity jackets. This kid appears to be about twenty-five but I didn't open his passport so I really don't know and it may be a high-quality counterfeit anyway but I know what he does for a living, all right. How do I know? Because it's what Bertrand did. He wouldn't ever tell me much directly, which in itself was a huge clue, and at first I had to fill in all the gaps in his e-mails, always from private servers, and mull the pauses when we spoke on the phone, always "restricted" caller ID, plus I never had a number to call him back. I remember all the calls, though—I always remembered them—and one satellite phone call still stands out.

"Dad, is that you?" It was Bertrand and he'd shouted above the roar of turbine engines and rattle of heavy armored metal vibrations in the background.

"Yes, I'm here," I replied, speaking with some urgency myself.

"I made it, Dad. They just extracted us."

"Were you successful?" I asked. I didn't ask for details; I knew better by then.

"Maybe," he answered.

"But you killed the enemy, right?"

"We killed somebody. That's all I really know."

"Where are you, Bertrand?"

"Here. I'm here."

"But where is 'here?'" There was a pause then and I imagined he was looking around, surveying the landscape, trying to soak it all in himself. "Is it dark where you're at?"

"Dad," he said. "Is this all there is?"

"You have to trust that you're doing what has to be done. I have to believe that too." There was another pause. "Bertrand, are you hurting?"

"Yes, I'm hurting," he said.

I'm about to speak to Stephen but I see that he's nodded off. I want to put the palm of my hand over his eyes, I even want to cry but a man doesn't cry and I don't think there's anything wrong with being a man, I really don't. I know Stephen is a man, that's why he's doing what he does. It's why Bertrand did too. It's not necessarily even patriotism.

I let Stephen be. If he wanted to talk he would have talked. It's just that I want to tell him I understand where he's at, that I know what he's doing. "I thank you for your service?" I want to say "God speed" even though I know there is no God. But mostly, I want to tell him to get the fuck out before it's too late. I'm the chorus in a Greek play and I have to anticipate the future, to warn him. I want to be helpful, that's all, yet who am I to tell this young man anything. Every man's destiny belongs to him and him alone. His life is his. Mine is mine. Bertrand's was Bertrand's.

Stephen wakes in twenty minutes and turns his head slowly; his eyes adjust to the fluorescent lighting and I wait for him to speak first. Babies are so cute when they wake; they roll their mouths and with their little fists they rub their eyes, then a smile dawns like a soft sunrise and only then do their eyes connect with yours. I want it all to happen right now but I know that's crazy. Stephen stands, takes a deep breath, and does smile, but almost curtly. He stretches and stands even straighter, he appraises me briefly but he won't remember me, and then he walks smartly out the door. I wait a few moments and then I step outside, too, and look for the Departures monitor. But why do I want to know where he's headed? Why do I think I should know, *can* know? I look for him but do not see him.

My shift runs its course easily enough. A couple of young men in uniform sign in, they're traveling together, and they spend all their time on their cell phones. I offer to get them a snack—"Microwave popcorn? Jonathan apple? Hot Pockets?"—and they politely decline. "Would you like to see what's on TV?" They shake their heads. It's OK. I'm invisible again.

I put the top down on my Mustang on the way home—the air is cool, the sky is black, and a state trooper slowly passes me on my left and we nod to each other. Up the highway a few minutes later I see that he's pulled someone over and I change lanes. Soon a loud motorcycle comes up from behind and rouses me from that place where I was.

CHAPTER 4

I worked in a bicycle shop when I was a teenager, nothing I ever put on a résumé, but it was a real job from a time when a boy could walk into a store and talk to the owner (the owner was always in the store then, before franchisers and big box stores took over everywhere) and he'd size you up and maybe give you a chance, teach you a lot, too, if you were willing to learn, which I was. Even today you can ask me anything about Schwinn bicycles when they were still made in America, the ones with heavy steel tubing like plumbers' stock and Sturmey-Archer three-speed hubs "Made in England," which sounded both exotic and regal at the time. I helped younger kids who'd "popped" a tire on a nail or bent a rim when they jumped a curb, even taught some to adjust those Sturmey-Archer hubs which was as tricky as setting the spring on a mouse trap. I still ride, own a Cannondale from when they were made in the USA too. I ride on the Monon Greenway, a rails-to-trails conversion that runs from the northern suburbs to downtown Indianapolis, runs on an old single-track commuter line that's been paved over for the purpose. Lots of old telephone poles remain on the sides of the rail bed leaning this way and that, a few still with their colored glass insulators, and the flora in the drainage ditches is as diverse as the past passengers who spat out seeds and stones from open windows in summer. I prefer the trail because so much of America can be seen from it, the kiddie pools and dog runs in the backyards of modest split-level homes, an iron trestle bridge still in use over a busy thoroughfare, and old industrial buildings with large windows that lighted the workshop floors in the days when factories shook from the heavy machine-age tooling. And my favorite, a still active lumberyard where you can savor the sweet burnt fresh smell of sawdust. It's early on a Thursday morning and I don loose-fitting mesh basketball shorts and a yellow T-shirt because I am going for a ride. I don't wear stretch Lycra with chamois pads for my butt and I don't have special bicycle shoes that lock onto the pedals for speed. I'm no boy racer, but I do ride with drop handlebars, which is cheaper than Pilates for my back and just as effective. The roundtrip is thirty-two miles up and down from where I live, a plenty good workout for someone my age.

"What is your fitness goal?" the nurse in my doctor's office asked me a couple of years ago.

"That's it," I'd replied.

"What's it?"

"I want to be fit. That's my fitness goal."

I ride two or three times a week, depending on the weather. If it's hot I don't mind because "dripping wet" is a perverse pleasure and if it's cool I wear fleece over stretchy ski tights and gauntlet gloves against the wind. And I occasionally swim in the indoor pool at the Y and I belong to a senior softball league. Hiking in a nearby county park too.

"But what part of your body are you most interested in?" the nurse had persisted.

I didn't answer that one right away; I just offered up my best Johnny Carson deadpan look and waited for her to break first, which she did, and we both had a laugh. "Come on, you know what I mean, Mr. Bogdanovic," she said.

"Cardiovascular," I finally announced. "Heart and lung. That's what's most important."

As the weather is pleasant on this day—fair skies, calm air, and temperature like a light throw—a lot of people are out on the Monon, especially for a weekday. I don't mind the vitality of it all but I thread a line between women pushing prams and kids on their wobbly hover boards, then I stand on the pedals to get away from the madding crowd.

Halfway through my ride into town I need a break so I detour into a trendy, upscale neighborhood known as Broad Ripple Village. Everyone knows the type of neighborhood— Fair Trade, natural fiber, and handmade-apparel stores, modern dance and yoga studios, art galleries that support local artists, nightclubs and "pubs," not bars, and, basically, doesn't anyone have a real job anymore? I can't complain, though—I'm getting my Social Security before it runs out, which is more than these kids can expect. I stop at a coffee shop and park my bike between the teeth of a giant comb that is laid horizontally on its spine—they call it an art installation—and a sign inside says the staff grinds its own beans, maybe even picks them in Kenya or Honduras themselves, but the main thing is that it's not a Starbucks. This neighborhood is too hip, too arty, for a Starbucks. I'm one of the regulars and I order iced tea when it's my turn in the queue.

"Hi, Dwight," the barista says to me. A young, lean black woman with tightly braided hair, Tanesha has told me she's an education major at Butler University, which is only two miles away.

"How are the applications going?" I ask. Tanesha will be a senior and she needs to do her student teaching in the fall.

"They're all courting me," she replies.

"You know why, don't you?" I say.

"Well, forget you, too, Mr. Dwight," she says as she hands me my iced tea.

It's all in jest, or at least I hope it is. But I don't think kids today really hate older people per se. They just hate older people who act old. If you're Betty White with a great attitude, or Bill Clinton with a reputation for still being sexy, then it's all right. Maybe I'm just everyone's favorite crotchety old uncle. I notice a section of the *New York Times* in a booth, only slightly mangled, and I slide onto the bench seat. More regulars come in. One, Bernie, spots me and sidles up without asking. Bernie's almost as old as I am and he owns quite a lot of rental property in the area. He's been after me to come work for him for some time—keep an eye on his holdings, make sure all the inspections are up-to-date, watch those three-hour lunch breaks his office staff likes to take, things like that.

"But what would you do with all your free time?" I asked him the last time he brought it up.

"I know this young dancer, she likes to swim nude," he replied then. "I'd go with her every day to the nudist resort in Centerville."

Broad Ripple was a blue-collar, working-class neighborhood at a time in America when that was all quite respectable. Simple frame homes up and down the side streets, front lawns with white picket fences at the property line, and kids who skipped rope on the sidewalks after school. Mom and Pop grocery stores with living quarters on the second floor lined the main commercial street, as did real butcher shops, the meat cutters in long white aprons, and plump sausages and plucked chickens hanging from overhead rods, as well as real diners offering low-cost lunches instead of low-fat yogurt shops. There always were bars, but only ones with big Schlitz globes out front or neon Carling Black Label signs in the windows. But no craft beers, no Stella Artois and so on.

"Enough of this already," I tell myself. I'm romanticizing things and I don't want to be a person who always thinks about the way things were, to become mired in sentimentality, ossified in my own brittle past. I wouldn't mind knowing more about this young dancer who likes to swim nude, I admit, but even that might be just another old fart kind of thing I need to exorcise from my mind. I am not an old fart. Write one hundred times on the chalkboard, "I am not an old fart."

My tea has an oddly misplaced impression of coconut and I wonder if Tanesha spiked it, so to speak, or maybe it's the daily special. I usually like orange pekoe, straight, no chaser. I look up at the menu board above the back bar and I see the sign, "Flavored teas no extra charge on Thursdays," and I sigh. Bernie asks me what's wrong so I must have a sour expression on my face.

"Nothing," I tell him. "You should try this tea. It's really good."

Bernie's full name is Bernard Goldberg, like the veteran TV journalist, and I guess it is a bit of a stereotype that he's into rental property. No slums, though—yuppies pay their rent, don't want trouble, and leave their units clean when they move out. I've never seen Bernie get too ethnic either. I don't know if he prays three times a day, five times, or only once a year. I don't care about his dietary habits. Thetis used to say the Jews were God's chosen people but Bernie has told me that's not quite right. God offered his law to all the peoples of the Earth and lots accepted it, but on condition. "What's in it for us? What do we get in return?" they asked. I guess they didn't know who they were dealing with. But the Jews, the ancient Jews, accepted His law unconditionally.

That's why they were chosen. It's not like God looked at all the peoples of Earth and thought that the Jews were the best and *consequently* awarded them. At least that's what Bernie says. Bernie used to be a rabbinical school student, he told me. "Most of my friends, they either kept the faith, joined a law firm, or became Communists. Me? I didn't abandon one cult just to join another." Bernie has a new proposal for me, a short-term project, minimal travel, and pays well, he says.

Am I interested? he wants to know.

I'm thinking, "Probably not," but he tells me anyway. Bernie needs a man in Chicago. That's how he puts it too—"a man in Chicago." He's been looking at property up in the Albany Park area on the Northwest Side; it's becoming a lot like Broad Ripple Village, he says. Albany Park was formerly a solidly white and very middle-class neighborhood with lots of single-family brick homes with large front parlors and bay windows but also nice three-flats and six-flats, nice city parks with tennis courts and public swimming pools too. The main attraction today, though, is that it's on the Brown Line rapid transit and all the millennials are abandoning cars in favor of bicycles and public transportation. Bernie says they've been priced out of neighborhoods closer to downtown or nearer the lake so they're starting to look at Albany Park. He wants me to walk the streets and talk to people, look at the cars and the customers going in and out of stores. Monitor the police runs, too, and see if people look over their shoulders as they unlock the doors to their homes and apartments. Abandoned cars stripped of their license plates, hood ornaments, even their wheels? Signs of trouble, like signs of progress, could be anywhere.

"Prices are rising," Bernie says. "I don't do algorithms like they do on Trulia but there must be a formula for these things. A guy could win a Nobel Prize if he could figure it out. Or at least get rich."

Most people in Indianapolis have been to Chicago many times. The lakefront, the museums, the shopping—it's the Big Leagues and Indianapolis is Triple A at best. There used to be regular train service between the two cities but now it's down to three times a week and you leave at midnight or something like that, then a long layover in Crawfordsville or wherever. I'd been to Chicago only once; landmarks to me then were the ivy-covered outfield walls of Wrigley Field, which I'd seen plenty of times on television, the small yachts and skiffs lilting left and right in the Lake Michigan harbor, and especially the architecture. I ask myself why I'd never thought of living in Chicago. Perhaps it was resentment. Here I was, stuck in Indianapolis, "no mean city," Benjamin Harrison once said, but if you need to say it maybe there is some question, sour grapes behind the brash words. I'd once thought of visiting Chicago a second time, though, making a kind of pilgrimage so I could see the Biograph Theater where John Dillinger was betrayed—did you know he's buried in a section of Crown Hill Cemetery in Indianapolis not far from where my son is interred? They both were local boys yet one is more familiar to the nation than the other.

I know why Bernie has lobbied me to join his team. I'd previously told him of my days selling encyclopedias door-to-door when I was younger, of my "passion" for the untethered lifestyle at the time. I never claimed that I made much money at it but Bernie said that didn't matter. I just think he realized it takes a certain kind of person to go up to a stranger and insinuate himself into the other person's life, to let the scornful looks bounce off your hide like so many artillery shells off an armored tank. To get people to like you, which is almost a necessary condition of closing any sale.

See, I'd dropped out of Indiana State University in 1968 and begun selling knowledge, not buying. Basically I didn't like higher education. I'd begun to feel like I was still in high school, or even middle school, like I was this big kid who'd been forced to sit with children. They even had you sit on metal chairs with laminated armrests and you sat facing a teacher who stood in front of a Dry-Erase board and the thing is, here's the real thing, none of the other students minded. They just wanted it to be over with. Not waiting to hear the bell ring after fifty minutes, but for four years to be over. What was I studying that would keep me in my seat? Human psychology and American literature, plus an elective in résumé writing? I did enjoy my two philosophy classes—I'd thought about majoring in the subject but that only prepares you to sell encyclopedias and you don't need a degree to do that anyway. College was a deferment from the Vietnam War and I think my father had mixed feelings about what I was doing but I felt guilty because I'd read *The Trial and Death of Socrates*, there being no room for doubt once you've made your commitment to citizenship. However, I was diagnosed with mild scoliosis which gave me a 1-Y deferment, meaning I was low priority for the military draft after all. I dropped out of school and took a job selling encyclopedias for Britannica plus some newfangled teaching machines—the machines were based on the programmed learning theories of B. F. Skinner, whom I had studied in my psychology class. *Do this, don't do that; that's the wrong answer, repeat after me, that's the right answer. You learn by reinforcement.* I'd gotten the idea to try sales from Eugene O'Neill's *The Iceman Cometh*, which I'd read in a literature class, so maybe there was value to a college education after all.

"Boy, how much money you got in yo' pocket?" the man asked. That's how the sales meeting began and the answer from a man on my right was, "Not much." It was late summer, no central air-conditioning in the older downtown Terre Haute hotel and about nine or ten of us sat in metal banquet chairs, some with torn vinyl over the yellowed foam padding, and the man, he called himself "the director," (as in dye-REC-toh), had loosened his tie as sweat beaded on his brow and soaked the underarms of his white shirt. A large pedestal fan, the kind with a round-wire housing to protect you from the blades, rattled as it pushed the air our way but not much reached us. We were in Banquet Hall C, "The Pomegranate Room," and though it was not a large room, still it was too large for the nine or ten of us and the high ceiling must have made us look like specimens in a glass jar, a human terrarium. That's not how I felt at the time, though—I'd polished my best leather shoes and I'd pressed my Levi's 501s, plus I wore a silky shirt with an outlandish collar that looked like floppy dog ears. These things were stylish in 1968, I guess, and I wanted to make a good impression. I was going to learn how to sell encyclopedias.

The director told us he'd come up from Louisiana, that he'd sold educational tools all over the southland and now he was going to do the same for the Middle West, which the boys at corporate told him would be his new territory. "'Errol,' they told me, 'do for the people in Indiana what you done for your home in Louisiana,'" he said. Errol added that he was originally from Baton Rouge, but couldn't testify that he was conceived there, a joke that drew a couple of laughs from the men but also embarrassed and chagrined expressions from the women present. Errol had set up a table with a complete set of encyclopedias on one side and the teaching machine on the other; the latter looked a lot like a mimeograph, same industrial grey finish over the thin metal housing, even a crank at the side where you turned the pages.

"Ask me anything," Errol said at one point. "You, you boy, what's on yo' mind that you just gotta know but don't have the time to look up, you just couldn't get to the library to do that." Errol was looking at me and I was kind of dumbstruck, then everyone else turned in their chairs to look at me. I wasn't self-conscious so much as caught by surprise; nevertheless, I took his question at face value. Yes, sir, there were so many things I wanted to know but so few ways to find out. I pondered the question for a few seconds and finally asked if Ben-Hur was a real person; I asked about Ben-Hur because I knew that the man who'd written the book was from Indiana and I'd seen the movie, of course, but I just didn't know what was real and what not.

"Was Ben-Hur a real person?" Errol repeated with great fanfare, leaning forward with his hands on his hips. "Well, I don't know. How would I know somethin' like that? But I tell you what. I'll look it up right here in my genuine faux-leather-bound and gold-tone-embossed *Encyclopaedia Britannica*." He'd already picked up a volume stamped "Bayeu-Ceanothus" on the spine but as he thumbed through the pages he looked up and declared, "Now, how do you spell that name?" He said it with a smile and everyone laughed this time.

"Yep, I've got it right here, right at my fingertips," he continued. He tapped the page several times with the pad of his right index finger. "Says right here, *Ben-Hur: A Tale of the Christ*, is a novel by Lew Wallace published by Harper & Brothers in 1880. The story recounts in descriptive detail the adventures of Judah Ben-Hur, a fictional Jewish prince from Jerusalem who is enslaved by the Romans at the beginning of the first century and becomes a charioteer and a Christian."

Errol looked up at me and at the others seated nearby and it was only then that I realized what he reminded me of—it was an itinerant Southern preacher at a tent rally. "Well, we have the answer, don't we?" Errol continued. "Fictional means not true, like somethin' that's made up. I don't think the part about Jesus was made up, but I never read about no Judah Ben-Hur in the Bible. Any Jewish people here? Maybe he's in the *Gemara*. I think that's what the Jews call their holy books. But if the *Encyclopaedia Britannica* says it's fiction, well, that's as good as Gospel itself." With that he slammed the volume shut, not in anger, but with finality; he'd proven his point, hadn't he.

Errol explained that this was one of the best sales techniques to use once out in our territory—"Tell the dubious housewife or the skeptical retiree to ask you anything, 'Just go ahead, I'm not afraid, whatever's on your mind,' and when they do they almost always will say something like, 'Well, all right, but just one question and then will you go away?' Then when they ask you somethin' you mull it for a while and then you tell them, 'Madam or Sir, I have no idea what the right answer is. I have absolutely no freakin' idea. But look here. I got this set of books and I know it's got the answer.' Then you point to your little cart, what's got all your volumes, and you pull out the right one. 'What's your question again?' you ask 'em. That's just to be friendly—you tell them that of course you remember the question. And then you look it up. 'Yep, here it is. Babe Ruth hit his 714th home run on May 25, 1935, at Forbes Field in Pittsburgh, Pennsylvania.' If they look impressed, or even if they don't, you can add that Ruth was a member of the Boston Braves then, that you're givin' 'em that information for free. Of course, not everyone is gonna ask about baseball. That's just an example."

At home after the meeting, I'd already sold all my old textbooks and a slide rule, too, to a student-run bookstore that was set up in the basement of an apartment building off campus, mind your head and turn left at the boiler, I lay back on my bed and I watched on my nine-inch black-and-white portable TV a series of events as they unfolded in Chicago. It was the time of the 1968 Democratic National Convention and the height of the Vietnam War protests.

"The whole world is watching. The whole world is watching," protesters chanted in front of a phalanx of police as they rallied across from the Conrad Hilton Hotel on Michigan Avenue, which was where many of the delegates stayed during the convention.

"Hey, hey, LBJ, how many kids did you kill today?" I remember that chant too.

One camera followed a solitary woman as police chased her up the long, Forum-like steps of the Art Institute; she stumbled halfway up and crashed to her knees and hands. Two policemen grabbed her from behind and hauled her back down the steps. In another shot I could see a policeman chase a reporter down an alley. How did I know he was a reporter? The man held up his press pass like a superstition symbol and waved it frantically in front of his pursuer, who beat him with his stick anyway. Smoke and haze gathered above the heads of all the protesters and the night had a ghostly air about it, especially on a low-resolution black-and-white TV screen. It looked like people fleeing a hurricane, but the hurricane had a face and a helmet on top of its head. They were culling the herd.

FOR THE next eighteen months I sold encyclopedias door-to-door in small towns throughout the Midwest and parts of the Great Lakes region, being denied more times than Jesus, meeting only women who wanted a ticket out of town, *The Postman Always Rings Twice* kind of action, or young girls who already were pregnant but might want to pin it on me. I was an itinerant who stayed in independent motels, the kind that were nothing but a row house with eight or ten rooms side by side like a chicken coop, or in older "tourist courts," the kind with individual cottages and mobile home lots for rent, too, "full hook-up included," the latter typically let to older people who maybe had a pet dog that ate scraps from the nearest dumpster, or to people who had clay flower pots they liked to put in their windows but no known living relatives anywhere. Or I stayed in mysterious little towns like Frontera, Illinois, that were way, way off the grid. Yes, I collected a few stories that I might tell in later years but most had no more value than confederate money saved in a shoebox.

Let me tell you about just one episode from that period in my life. I fondly recall "Gordon the Bookseller" from Frontera, population 1,311. Gordon Jones was a seventh-grade math and science teacher who ran a bookstore on the town square a couple of afternoons a week and on Saturdays as a public service; I was staying at an old hotel up the street at the time I met him. I stopped into the bookstore while reconnoitering prospects on the town's Main Street, such as it was, and I noticed a middle-age man sitting in an easy chair behind the front window of his store. The man reminded me of Arnold Palmer—same acrylic knit cardigan, same polyester blend pants with a self-adjusting belt, same widow's peak hairline—yet the man was more like soft white bread than world-class athlete.

"Greetings," I said as I entered the small bookstore. I carried a boxy sample case in those days along with a couple of full sets of encyclopedias I kept in the trunk of my car and Gordon immediately pegged me as a salesman. "Don't worry," I told him as he offered up only a doubtful expression. "No Fuller brushes here. Not even a better mousetrap.

I've got knowledge here." I tapped the side of the vinyl-clad case.

"If it's something I need I already got it, young man," he replied. The front of the store was set up like a day room, two upholstered chairs and little tables on a large Oriental-style carpet, a towering ficus and a potted bamboo palm tree on either side of a beige slipcovered sofa, and check-out was on a nicked Formica stand with a sparkly finish. I took a seat opposite the man and put down my case.

"You like reading, obviously," I said, looking past him toward a couple of freestanding bookcases and a book display on a small folding card table. "Your customers must like reading, too, or they wouldn't be your customers."

"You a book salesman?"

"It's sort of a calling for me."

"What kind of books do you distribute? I won't carry pornographic titles."

I had to laugh. "I don't either, but we'd both be a lot richer if we did."

Well, that broke the ice, sort of, but Gordon the Bookseller wasn't interested in encyclopedias. He had several old sets of *World Book* and one *Collier's* collection and he said he sometimes let kids come in and consult them without paying anything. "Most of what's in encyclopedias never changes," he said. "The Civil War is the Civil War; Julius Caesar is Julius Caesar. Any science they might learn likely will change by the time they start college."

It was a warm afternoon in Frontera, the overhead fans in the store not functioning, and so I asked Gordon for a drink of water. I felt I was in a Tennessee Williams play, or in the South generally—everyone's suspicious of you at first but they act friendly enough until they're sure one way or another. It's only when they conclude you're up to no good

that they'll run you out of town, due process being a scorned
lover. Gordon proved to be very gracious, offering iced tea
from a pitcher in his refrigerator instead of water.

"So how long you been on the road?" he asked me after
we'd both settled into our seats again. It had been about a
year, I told him.

"We don't see many strangers in Frontera. We're kind
of off the grid, you might say. Brigadoon without the songs.
A bus carrying some Double-A ballplayers from Rockford
broke down here once and all the girls flooded the local bars
when they heard about it but that's the extent of excitement
around here. Well, except for that murder. Maybe you heard
about it?"

Did Tennessee Williams write about actual murders in his
hazy backwater hamlets? Gordon proceeded to tell me about
a young drifter who'd gotten off the Trailways bus when it
stopped at the Sinclair Gas Station across from the old mor-
tuary and booked a room in the Frontera Guest House. "Is
that where you're staying?" Gordon asked. I nodded in the
affirmative.

This other young man, John Chance Whittaker he'd
called himself, went up and down the streets of Frontera
offering handyman services and day labor and even "will
work for food," but no one would hire him. Maybe it was the
long scar on his left cheek, or his blotchy hair like a rabid dog
that he tried to cover with a greasy cap yet always removed
when he'd introduce himself so everyone knew what, if not
why. I was about to ask about John Chance Whittaker's teeth
when Gordon volunteered information about that, too, surprising information. "They were really white," he said. "I
mean Sherwin-Williams high-gloss premium-enamel white,
and as straight as flagpoles. How do you figure an outlaw
renegade scavenger human being like that could have such

good teeth? Most people around here don't see a dentist until they got an abscess."

I had good teeth and I thought maybe I should hide them, speak with my lips closed. White teeth are the sign of the devil—was that it? I asked when the murder occurred, as well as who was murdered. I told Gordon I was from Indiana, as if it was a three-day donkey ride across the Wabash River and through the Shawnee Forest just to get there.

"So you never heard about the murder?"

"No, sir."

Gordon stroked his chin and reached for his iced tea. "Well, I guess murders are a daily occurrence in Indianapolis. They are in Chicago."

Here's what John Chance Whittaker is alleged to have done. "It was out by the railroad yard," Gordon told me. "Oh, sure, we knew that teenagers liked to sneak into the old box cars at night and either drink beer or fool around. The smart ones would bring in bales of hay and make a bed of it before they got down to business. We could add up the activity by the amount of fresh hay. The police would patrol the yard but they couldn't go through every box car every night, like on the hour every hour. It was one of the teens who reported finding Melissa Street lying half naked in one of those box cars, though, utterly lifeless and about sixty-five degrees body temperature. He was a good kid; he didn't freak out or anything. Just got back in his pickup and drove straight to the police station. There were no signs of a struggle or defensive wounds on the girl, but the autopsy revealed that she had had recent sexual relations. They found some smack in her system as well as a high blood alcohol level, but the coroner ruled it was death by asphyxiation. That means someone smothered her. That's why they called it a murder, not an accidental overdose though you can see how

doing drugs and drinking alcohol can lead to a person being
murdered. You can see that, right? What's your name again?
Dwight, yeah."

I nodded; no way I was going to challenge this man. I
did ask how old the girl was.

"Sixteen," Gordon said. "You know what that means."

"In Illinois?"

"Yep, it's still below the age of consent. They were going
to get this Whittaker fellow on both statutory rape and first-
degree murder."

I asked if the police had found any link between the girl
and suspect at the scene.

"Didn't need to. The police had a witness who'd testify
he overheard the two planning to meet there."

"Why didn't they just do it in the Frontera Guest House?
The suspect had a room there, right?"

"Well, you are a pathetic little fool, aren't you? Don't
you be trying your hand at a life of crime. You won't be any
more successful at it than you are at selling encyclopedias.
They'd be seen, Dwight. They'd be seen. That was why."

Gordon said that since the horrible crime the whole
town had been kind of sour on strangers. "People look at
you funny?" he asked me. I told him I'd just checked into the
hotel, paid cash, and was satisfied that my room was clean
though I wished the windows had screens. There was no
air-conditioning available anywhere in this town apparently.

"That hotel is mostly for folks on welfare, you know,"
Gordon said. "Didn't they tell you that? That's how it stays
open. The state pays for them. I say bring back the county
farm. Let them grow their own vegetables."

I wanted to ask Gordon when the next stagecoach out
of town might be leaving but I wasn't sure he'd appreciate
my levity, then I wondered if any of this tale was even true.

I'd been sitting in the bookstore for at least a half hour and there were no customers, not even a phone call. I thanked the man for the tea and then he told me it wasn't free, that I should pay him seventy-five cents. I gave him a dollar bill and hesitated before asking for change. But the man did give me a lead. "We got a library in the police station annex, just one room with a few desks for the people. It's open right now. They only open it once or twice a week. You might make a sale there."

The library was two blocks down and then left so I hefted my sample case and headed there. I didn't expect to find a Carnegie Library in the Craftsman or Neo-Classical style, but I wasn't thinking pole barn either. The entire police station and the so-called annex were sheathed in corrugated steel on the outside; only two walls had windows and the stairway to the police station proper was little more than a prefab concrete fixture, what you can buy at Home Depot for fifty-nine dollars. The annex had its own entrance, a narrow nine-lite door, and a stepstool like in a mobile home leading up.

"Why, hello," said the large woman who was seated behind a steel desk in the middle of the room. It was just a student desk, the kind you could buy at a discount or office supply store, comes in a box and you attach the legs yourself; one side has a lap drawer and there's a small file cabinet in the single pedestal, and the top is just vinyl over chipboard. The woman, pleasant enough in demeanor and dressed in a Hawaiian-print muumuu, looked ridiculous sitting behind it. "May I help you?"

I surveyed the steel shelving along the walls, the four folding banquet tables with folding chairs, two sets on either side of the librarian, plus a wall-mounted magazine rack in a corner. A bank of long fluorescent tube light bulbs hummed overhead. "You look pretty well stocked for a small-town library," I offered. "Where do you keep your encyclopedia?"

"Look closer," the woman said. "We have a set that one of the supermarkets in Belleville donated. The kind they give away for ninety-nine cents with a bag of groceries each week."

❖ ❖ ❖

I THANK Bernie for his offer and tell him I'll sleep on it. Once outside again I roll out my bicycle from the rack and mount it but before I head back to the trail I pause to look around. I do see people, I see cars, and I see life. Yet what I'm sensing just then is that I occupy a spot on this planet called Earth, latitude and longitude given, and if you were to look closely, very closely, like gods might be able to see us, it would be me here alone, not because I feel alone but because I am alone, in all the universe and throughout all of history it is I, and I alone, who have come to occupy this particular place and time.

CHAPTER 5

$\sim\sim$

It was cool the day I drove up to Chicago, having decided to investigate further Bernard Goldberg's offer of temporary employment. I didn't need the money, not that I'm rich, but I am fortunate in having everything I need to survive. I remember when Bill Clinton had his heart surgery and Hillary Clinton said she wished everyone had the same quality health insurance he had. Well, I have Medicare Parts A through Z and I don't need heart surgery. Or diabetes medicine or any of the products I see advertised on the nightly network news, those drugs with made-up names that always contain a "z" or "x" or "j" in them, sometimes in combination, computer-generated names because there is irrefutable statistical evidence that drugs with a "z" or "x" or "j" in the name sell better, not necessarily treat illnesses better. I'm expecting some newborn at the hospital to be named Xeljanz or Januvia any day now.

I've decided to take the Indiana Tollway, aka The Skyway, into the city, in part because the view from on high is better, more treetop level, and in part because the route passes right by Gary, where Grandpa lived. I did a little research and learned that United States Steel still has its "works" there, including four blast furnaces and three bottom-blown oxygen-process vessels. I know what the former are, but not the latter. Still it sounds hot in there. I've read that steel workers make at least $125,000 a year these days; Grandpa never brought home loot like that, I'm sure. I've also read that Americans are among the most productive workers in the world, which supposedly justifies the high salaries, but that's only because most of our remaining industries are heavily automated anyway. It's why United States Steel can pay people $125,000 to push buttons.

Though I'd been to Gary as a boy I'd not seen it in decades, only read the occasional apocalyptic narratives that have emerged from the rubble of its history. But Gary as seen from the Skyway looks like it once was formidable— I see the domed city hall, a little replica of ancient Rome itself, plus smokestacks like giant artillery pieces aimed at the warring gods themselves, and there's still the South Shore Line below the highway that has long connected the city to its patron saint Chicago. The rails glint under the sun, their lines are smooth and elegant, *essential*. Maybe I should pull off and look for Grandpa's old house, or Michael Jackson's boyhood home, I tell myself. But there's not enough life left in Gary to pull me off course. I'm on a quest; I can hear Chicago's thrum over the horizon.

I've been booked into the Renaissance Blackstone Hotel on South Michigan Avenue and upon arrival I recognize the nearby General Logan landmark from the 1968 convention riots. I pause and view the statue as if it's the monolith at the start of *2001: A Space Odyssey*, albeit without the Zara-thustra soundtrack, and then I move on. Once checked in to my hotel I find that I have a room facing the lakefront. It's late September and most of the small yachts in the harbor have dry-docked by now but not all and I enjoy the gentle cadence of their hulls as they bob and roll on the surface of the uneven sea, what looks like a sea to anyone from Central Indiana, and I look beyond their masts to the stoic light towers behind them just winking to life. My room is small with only a single bed and a little dresser but the wallpaper is textured and the walls themselves seem to be as thick as in an English castle so it all feels ample and as I stand at the window, the jacquard drapes pulled wide like opening night at the opera, I see the tips of waves flash like little lightning strikes and I strain to open the hotel window and lean out, to drink in deeply the cool evening air and suffuse myself with elemental ether; it's the first time since my youth that I wonder what it might be like to take flight. I think I'll sleep well, this, my first night in Chicago.

MY CONTACT is Judith Prime of Prime Real Estate and we are to meet near the Kimball Station, which is the terminus of the Brown Line in the heart of Albany Park. "Take the 'L,'" Prime told me. "You'll get to know the city better." I'd called her after having an expensive breakfast in the hotel restaurant and I know she's right. Prime explained that the route used to be called the Ravenswood Line, that old-timers still call it that, but the city fathers wanted to be more like London so they color-coded everything. "They should have asked a realtor," she said. "The London tube lines all have names, you know, not just colors."

Prime explained that she would be busy in the morning because she had two closings, business was that good, and I couldn't tell how old she was but her voice was a little smoky and she spoke with good diction, neither a Chicago accent (it's the nasal way they say "ah," especially in the name of the city) nor any kind of slack speech one often hears in Indiana below US 40. I pictured her with thick pancake makeup and heavy lip gloss, but I didn't really know. It's just how most female realtors I've known always looked.

It's the tail end of the morning rush hour but travelers still mill about the train platform, more disparate faces and implied stories than in a Norman Rockwell season of illustrations, old ladies lugging vinyl shopping bags but also well-dressed business types, natty woolen suits and Italian leather shoes and more. The morning is cool and the air is fresher than I might have expected in a big city, yet I recoil as a train approaches, then I realize it's just the clanging of railway couplings and brakes screeching that have startled me. Prime said it would take about twenty-five minutes to reach the terminus.

There are several free seats in the car and I take one near a window, two down from the automatic doors. I'm at ease as the train trundles on, across iron bridges and over the river, tight turns between densely packed buildings, yet at the Sedgwick Street station, about halfway through my trip, in steps a striking young woman, tall and loose-limbed and I can't help but look. She's wearing an alpaca sweater over yoga pants and her silver-dyed hair is cut concentration-camp-short on one side, hanging vines on the other, and her nasal septum is pierced by a nose ring with silver balls on the ends that remind me of a pawn shop symbol. Over her shoulder she's thrown a cotton canvas book bag. I look again at her yoga pants—she's turned partly away from me and her butt cheeks are tight and round like melons, and as she moves the book bag from one shoulder to the other while holding on to an overhead strap, her breasts swing and she catches me examining her but I don't flinch. I'm not ogling her at all. It's just that she looks a bit like Bertrand, same sleek body type and olive-toned skin—not quite Polynesian, perhaps Sicilian—and her nose, albeit mutilated by fashion, has the same long, narrow aspect as his, what they call aquiline in books. How could I ever explain to her what's really on my mind. She's a stranger and I'm just a strange man.

THE KIMBALL Station is not imposing, just a few ticket machines and turnstiles to enter and exit; I alight from the platform and land on Lawrence Avenue, the main commercial thoroughfare in the neighborhood. Looking up and down this street is not quite the same as being wowed by Michigan Avenue, though—there'll be no postcards highlighting this streetscape, no beauty shots from the Goodyear blimp during breaks in *Sunday Night Football* games, yet I discover a panorama that presents many possibilities, little specialty stores hawking kitchen utensils and lighting fixtures and vacuum cleaners, a halal butcher shop with cuts of meat dangling from hooks, as well as travel agencies that will help you get to Korea or Guatemala or Russia, not tourist destinations but the mother country in all cases. It's not at all like the 1950s in Indianapolis; this is Delancey Street on the Lower East Side of New York from one hundred years earlier brought up to date with signs stenciled in many foreign tongues, people hurrying up and down the sidewalk like schools of fish passing, and I see my roots in this procession too.

I walk west on Lawrence and after a couple of blocks I enter a gluten-free bakery but the inside is run-down, broken tiles on the floor and black-sheathed wires that hold cheap pendant lights dangle from the old coffered tin ceiling. The employees all have ponytails and big tats climbing up their arms and necks and those nose rings too. A young man working the counter acknowledges me.

"What'll you have?" he asks.

"What do you recommend?" I reply.

He looks down at the glass display case. "Oh, we have millet-chia rolls, some omega flax too. Are you new here?"

I'm surprised by the directness of the question but all he means is that he hasn't seen me before, I'm sure. I see some rolled cinnamon sticks in a glass jar and I point to them. "How long have you been open?" I ask.

"Two years," he says as he hands me my cinnamon stick. He's wrapped it in waxy tissue, which I appreciate.

"You've lasted the first six months. That's the hardest part, or so they say." I lick from my cinnamon stick, then crack the end in my mouth. "You the owner or just work here?"

The young man leans back against the wall and folds his arms across his chest, folds one leg across the other, too, and he cocks his head at an angle. "Are you from Michelin?" he asks.

I don't understand at first, then I realize he means the guide. It's a joke. "I'm working with a real estate investor," I say. "He's thinking of buying into the neighborhood."

"Push out the poor people, huh," the young man says.

I crack off another piece of my cinnamon stick. "Did *you* grow up here?" I ask.

The young man pushes off from the wall. "Touché," he says.

Other customers come in, they look the part, and I point a finger at the young man as I leave, one of those old school Frank Sinatra jazz club gestures, or was that De Niro? The young man seems to smile at me, then he fills an order for six cranberry wild rice buns, if I've heard correctly.

Once back on the street I begin to take note of the buildings themselves, not just the businesses that inhabit them. They're all two or three stories tall, red or yellow brick, many with terra-cotta trim, and some even have cloth awnings over the front plate-glass windows; I like those best, especially when the wind catches a valance. I may love walking in thick woods or across a golden meadow, I may like the crawl of moss green on the north side of a tree or the black blooming smell of soil after a heavy rain, the shape of the wind as it blows over a wheat field and the stillness of a deer before it bounds off in the distance, but buildings have lives and personalities, too, every building being home to so many stories.

As I continue walking I look up again and I see one sign for eyeglass repair and I think I might go up. I wear eyeglasses and they sit unevenly on the bridge of my nose which is why I never wear my glasses when I go for a bicycle ride. I have semi rimless frames with drilled lenses, what you'd see in the 1920s and '30s on doctors and lawyers and spinsters. Mine are fourteen-karat gold, very severe and all no-nonsense, but the temples wobble on the hinges and one of the original plastic nose pads is cracked and I think it is my good fortune to be walking down the street on a mild fall day in a new city and happen upon an eyeglass repair shop that can help me. I decide to go up.

Old books have a characteristic smell, not unlike dank basements—it's the mold—and vintage buildings have a bit of a uric acid smell, which is the wood studs decomposing over decades. I don't know how to describe the smell of Wetzlar Eyeglass Repair though. Dusty? Maybe it's the stale air in the one-room office with only a single door in and out, but it feels as if I've opened a chest in the attic that's been closed for a very long time. The Oriental-style carpet in front of the counter is well-worn and several travel posters from the 1920s and '30s have been tacked to the walls—streamlined stainless steel locomotives traveling through the Rockies, twin-engine airplanes over Argentina, the Eiffel Tower and City of Lights in broad and garish tints. An acrylic display case sits on one end of the front counter; it holds several samples of wire-rimmed and rimless eyeglass frames in both gold and silver and the proprietor sits at a lighted bench behind the counter. He doesn't look up when I come in. There is no cowbell but the floors creak a bit and it's not like he can have many customers in a day so he must be aware that someone has entered his space. I scan the office more critically and I spot a small oak cabinet with narrow drawers, something from an old hardware store perhaps, and I'm sure it's where he keeps his screws and bits and pieces. The proprietor is quite overweight and his thin hair hangs too low at the sides but his crown is bald, a true Friar Tuck look. He wears suspenders over a white oxford-cloth shirt that's open at the neck.

"Hello," I say as I approach the counter. The man doesn't immediately look up, but then he rises and comes forward, casting his head a little left and right while he studies me.

"Turn to the side," he says and I do. "Now the other way. Yes, I think I can help you."

The man has done this before. Put another way, why else would I have climbed the steps and ducked the latent cobwebs if I didn't need a repair? I remove my eyeglasses and hand them to the man.

"Art Craft," the proprietor says without looking up, and then he turns toward his bench. He continues speaking as he takes the few steps back to his seat. "That's American-made quality. The kids moving into the area come up here looking for them. Are you the original owner?" I tell the man I inherited the frame from my grandfather and that I'd started wearing them in the late 1960s after John Lennon and John Sebastian made similar ones popular again.

I'm struck by the man's baritone voice which is like an old-time radio announcer's only slightly buffeted by age. And business is apparently picking up—the alternative kids are into wire and rimless frames for sure. I've seen the trend even in Indianapolis.

I look more closely at the man's workbench. There's a mini torch, there are tiny screwdrivers, and there are magnifying glasses of assorted sizes. Order in chaos, I suppose. I ask him about the cracked plastic nose pad, which I think will be the hardest part to fix, and he reaches for a pair of fine metal snippets on a tray and he tells me that he can pry the old part out easily enough and install a piece from New Old Stock he's saved for instances like this. "I may have to use a little heat on one of the hinges," he says. "It's bent way out of shape. A wonder you can even see out of these things."

I laugh but it's mostly to be courteous. Then I ask the man how long he's been in business. He straightens up and points over my shoulder. "They interviewed me for the paper not too long ago," he tells me. "There's the clipping on the wall. Just the local alternative press but it gets read. They didn't even try to sell me ad space afterward like the big papers would do."

I turn around and read the article, which includes a couple of photos. "Joseph Baumgartner opened his shop on May 8, 1965, exactly twenty years to the day after the Allied victory in Europe. His father, Hugo Baumgartner, had emigrated from his native Germany in 1936 where he had worked on optics for Leica cameras. During the war he helped develop gunsights for the United States Army. 'I used to tinker with his old prototypes after the war,' Joseph said. 'Then he gave me his copy of Isaac Newton's treatise on *Opticks*.'" One of the pictures in the tear sheet shows a vintage black-and-white photograph of Joseph standing on the street just below where we are, he's much younger then, dark straight hair cleanly parted on the side and a wide smile across his otherwise anodyne face.

Mr. Baumgartner is finished in about ten minutes and he reaches for a ball point pen and a small receipt book and he itemizes the work he's done, then he rises again and presents me with both my eyeglasses and the bill. The tally is sixty-two dollars and I guess he can read the confusion, or is it annoyance, on my face.

"It's the article in the paper," he says. "I raised my prices after that."

Now it was time to meet Miss Judith Prime. She'd texted me about eleven A.M. to say she was just wrapping up her second closing but the realtor for the other side was being an "ASS," her word, all caps. She suggested we meet at a coffee shop on Kedzie Avenue across from the Brown Line stop, which was the one just before the terminus. "Hop on the 'L' again or walk. It's not far either way," she'd added. It was a fairly long text for someone who was hurrying through a real estate closing, I thought, as I scrolled through it, then I simply replied "OK." I decide to walk, and when I reach Kedzie I come across a US Army Recruiting Station. It's just a small office behind a plate-glass display window, banks of fluorescent tube lighting set in the acoustical tile ceiling, and there is a single door leading in. Posters of proud soldiers in digital camo uniforms and combat helmets looking bravely outward and upward line the walls and there are others that announce, "There's Strong, and There's Army Strong." And then there are the "earn money for college" pitches. Brochures are stacked on a wire rack and a recruiter sits at a small steel desk reading something; he doesn't notice me as I stop at the window to stare inside.

Bertrand and I had gone to a recruiting station like this, which was near a big shopping center in Indianapolis. He was just seventeen so I had to go with him to sign him up. The afternoon we went—I took off work and he left school early, with or without permission, I didn't ask—and there were a couple of other recruits at the office when we got there, a young black male but not so young as Bertrand and a guy in his thirties who was asking about the reserves. We waited in chairs along one wall and, in fact, I'd begun leafing through a recruiting brochure. There wasn't much to talk about with Bertrand because I knew all along he'd be going in and I think he knew I knew. It was in the way he'd discuss famous battles in history that might have come up in school or just in a movie—"What was the plan of attack; did the opposing generals know each other; did soldiers really write their last letters home before a battle just in case?"—and it was in some of the books he'd read, such as Norman Mailer's *The Naked and the Dead* and *Going after Cacciato* by Tim O'Brien, although neither was a gung-ho, go get 'em, John Wayne flag waver. Quite the contrary. It was just that Bertrand always took the side of those who would stand tall, who wouldn't let others take on more risk than he himself was willing to assume, which is how he understood manhood, how he figured his grandfather and great-grandfather understood it. I think it was exactly this egalitarian spirit that made me so proud of him and perhaps secretly ashamed of myself at the same time. The recruiter, a woman who looked like she could have been a young nursery school teacher or a pediatrician, went over the rules and responsibilities, talked about all the career options, and asked Bertrand about his grades and hobbies and even his favorite sports teams. He answered everything as if this were a real job interview, as if he wanted to be sure the army would accept him, as if there could be any doubt. Then she asked Bertrand why he wanted to join.

"Well, I don't know," he said after a slight hesitation, speaking in a voice that was at once solitary and staunch. "I just have to take a stand, you know?"

Once back home Thetis asked us how things went. "Millie's son is in Germany, you know," she said as she turned from him to me. "I think Dr. Kagan's son, too, but I don't know where he's stationed."

Thetis asked Bertrand when he'd be leaving for basic and what kind of training they'd be offering afterward, even whether he thought he might make a career of it. She asked the questions that someone who was really interested in his life would ask; they were not the kind of questions a worrier or controller would ask. But was she masking her own anxiety then? Even if she weren't a mother—*his* mother—she would have grasped the sensitivity of the moment, even felt the distant drums of war itself underneath her feet. Later that evening I heard Thetis whispering the much-maligned Serenity Prayer to herself: *God grant me the serenity to accept the things I cannot change, courage to change the things I can, and wisdom to know the difference.* The prayer sounds weak the first time you hear it, like something Nietzsche would ridicule, or Lenin, but its strength can only be appreciated when you see someone actually living a life in harmony with those words.

DIXON'S COFFEE Shop is like a colorful movie set, only it's authentic, and I suddenly realize how false old newspaper tear sheets and movies on the silver screen were because the

world always was in color, never black-and-white. I look at
the icons before me, the circular, chrome-trimmed barstools
with red seats that lined a sparkly laminated counter, as well
as the U-shaped booths by the windows that feature genuine
bark-brown Naugahyde vinyl and contrast piping along the
seams. And the little hexagonal tiles in the floor—nobody
lays them one by one anymore. All the lighting fixtures are
traditional, too, frosted glass globes and brass sconces, and
the waitresses wear red-and-white uniforms with little ruffles
across their bosoms. Looking closely at the countertop I see
the wear marks from the hot china plates thrown down over
the years and I know the place is real just because it is so very
old. I wonder if the new owners, when they come, and they
will come, they'll be sharp young lawyers from downtown
who know a good thing when they see it, and I wonder if
they will look in a catalog somewhere and order cheap made-
in-China reproductions in an effort to make this place look
more authentic than it already is. But today it is unmolested.

I glance at my wristwatch, I still wear one, a Seiko with
a clasp wristband, it's enough, and it's a quarter to twelve,
very nearly so. A waitress hurries over to me and asks, "How
many?" and I tell her I'm expecting someone. She points to
a far corner where I see a woman who seems to be settling
in; I see her adjusting her suit jacket at the shoulders and she
takes a deep breath, which I can tell from the way her chest
swells, and then she puts a cell phone to her ear.

"Perhaps this is the person," the waitress says. I try to
place her accent. I think she's Romanian—it's the way she
sounds a little like my grandfather, but softer. I thank her, I
actually bow, and I walk over to my lunch date.

"Miss Prime?" I say. She's seated at the end of the booth
near the aisle and I'm standing almost on top of her; the sun
is baking the other end of the table through the window.

"Dwight," she says brightly, slipping her iPhone into her purse as she looks up. "Did you have any trouble finding the restaurant?"

I sit down opposite her. "I've had a wonderful morning," I tell her. "I'm truly a tourist today."

Prime tells me that one of her closings has been delayed but it's only because of a technicality and she thinks the seller will come around. "Oh, real estate," she declares. "I don't know why I ever got into this business." The Romanian waitress comes by and takes our order—Prime orders a veggie omelet and black coffee, explaining that she didn't even have time for breakfast that morning, and I order a cheeseburger and fries, why not.

"Separate checks?" the waitress asks. I notice that she has one of those little paper receipt pads in her hand just like Baumgartner had, complete with a reusable carbon sheet to make duplicate copies. Miss Prime says the meal's on her and I demur at which point she reaches across the table and puts her hand on mine. "I love a man who doesn't feel he has to be bigger than a woman," she says. Prime has a wolf's-grey eye color, her lipstick is a blend of purple and pewter, and her skin is like soapstone, not pasty at all. I think she's in her early fifties, perhaps, and she's very lively, what we used to call vivacious.

"Have you been to Chicago before?"

"Just once, a long time ago."

"What do you think of our little town now?"

"It's a great city."

"Is it much like Indianapolis?"

"American cities are more and more alike, I think."

"It's the Internet, isn't it?"

"Well, there was TV before that, and picture magazines before that."

"You're funny, you know."

We enjoy our meal, which arrives quickly, but we also get down to business. Prime has a file with printouts from the Multiple Listing Service plus several reports from consulting firms all stamped "Confidential" in bold, block-like letters. She tells me that algorithms suggest Albany Park is eighteen to twenty-one months away from exploding. "And the report was completed in July so it'll be sooner than that," she says. "But you can just count the number of craft breweries and vegan restaurants in the zip code. Anyway the city is going to install six more bike-share racks along Lawrence and maybe the same on Foster Avenue. That's the heart of Albany Park. I can hear the footsteps getting closer every day."

We read while we eat; soon there are papers spread all over our table. Prime is shuffling through several before she reaches the one she wants. "Yes, here it is," she says, looking up. "What do you think of these numbers?" It's a bar graph showing the rise in both monthly apartment rents and closing prices for homes for the last several years—up 3 percent, then up 5 percent, then 8 percent. Prime calls it "almost exponential."

"Where do I sign?" I say. Prime looks at me quizzically. "I mean, I should buy everything that's for sale if the numbers are correct."

We spend the afternoon looking at single-family homes all dating from the 1920s that are on the market—I note that some still have their original leaded-glass windows—and an array of six-flat walk-ups that all are being converted to condominium sales. It's not so much that poorer people are being pushed out as money is pouring in to the neighborhood—so the irresistible force is stronger than the immovable object after all. By four P.M. or so we are finished and Prime says she has to go back to the office; when I tell her I

won't be returning to Indianapolis until the morning she suggests we get together for drinks that evening. She mentions a
nightclub near the Rush Street entertainment district, a place
called Wally's, and I tell her I'll find it.

"Nine o'clock?" I say.

BACK AT the hotel I feel that I have too many hours on my
hands. I go down to the hotel lounge for a drink.

The lounge is brassy and tinny at the same time, I think
it's because of the contractor-grade fixtures, but at least the
actual bar is highly polished, even ebony-like. I see the usual
assortment of businessmen and the chatter is not unpleasant,
more like the uneven cadence of a babbling brook amidst
the stirrings of a windswept forest; it's life too. I sidle up to
the bar and order my Scotch on the rocks, yet it's only a few
seconds before a woman in a short sequined dress slides onto
the seat next to me and places her patent leather purse right
against my elbow.

"Oh, I'm sorry," she says demonstratively. I study her face
before responding—her lipstick is like lacquer, her eyelashes
like cockroaches, and her teeth like pickets. I know what this
is all about and I try to stare her down but I'm not succeed-
ing. The woman is not that old yet she is easy to unmask.
I can see her coarse skin behind her heavily rouged cheeks
and I look down at her chest, which is full and puffy. I have
cash; I have one hundred dollars in my wallet, maybe more.
What do prostitutes charge these days, I wonder? It's not
something you can check on Angie's List or Yelp. It doesn't
matter what I'm thinking though. A burly man in a dark blue
suit steps between us and picks up the woman's handbag.

"This way, Sugar," he tells her, and he escorts the woman
out of the lounge but not before sneering at me. I don't like

the way the bartender is looking at me either—*What did I do?* I'm thinking—but why bother challenging these people? This is not my city. I finish my drink and leave.

Upstairs in my room I ask myself if I like myself. It was an episode of *Dr. Phil* on TV that prompted the question and I think it's not a bad one at all. Socrates said, to thine own self be true, and Dr. Phil asks if you like yourself. I see the connection; I'm not making fun of Dr. Phil. The prostitute may have been booted but I know there are others in Gotham, fresher fruit and comelier. I think of Thetis and I try not to feel guilty. She'd understand that men have "desires," which is how she defended Bill Clinton once, or maybe it was Gary Hart, same difference. Yet I never hurt Thetis that way when we were married and I did have opportunities. Every man who's halfway attractive, reasonably fit, and has all his teeth has opportunities. It wasn't just the betrayal of trust either. It's that you become a liar and have to arrange your schedule just so, then erase the telltale signs like a criminal destroying evidence after the fact. I didn't want to be that kind of person, two-faced, sneaky, smug. I wanted to like myself, basically.

I'd met Thetis while volunteering with my service club at a local women's shelter. That was at a time when the idea of a "women's shelter" was quite radical. The activists who ran the place—it was in an abandoned elementary school in an older, depressed part of town that the Board of Education leased to the group for one dollar a year—either were nuns, former nuns, ex-Peace Corp workers and VISTA Volunteers, or "known feminists" from a local university, as one vocal critic of the effort labeled them. Women, all claiming to have been abused by their spouses or boyfriends in some way, often up from Southern Indiana and even parts of Kentucky, but inner-city blacks as well, slept with their children on cots in various classrooms, one family to a class-room, and everyone ate in the school's cafeteria. The residents were expected to help clean—some would and some wouldn't—and the volunteers helped with tutoring, résumé writing, dress-for-success, and job skills. My service club was recruited to do some painting and make minor repairs to the steam heat as winter was approaching then; Thetis was one of two nurses from Saint Vincent Hospital who ran a first-aid clinic at the shelter. I was thirty at the time and belonged to the group in part for its Sunday afternoon softball league but also because we'd go out and drink after our monthly meetings. Seven of us spent a full Saturday that October volunteering—we brought with us big push brooms, several five-gallon containers of eggshell-white paint and rollers that a Lowe's home store had donated, a large floor sander that we rented, and, for some reason, spades and shovels. We must have thought we were the seven dwarfs.

Sister Josephine met us at the rear loading dock as we pulled up in our caravan which, if I remember correctly, consisted of a white Dodge commercial van, a red Chevy C-10 pickup, and my grey Ford Escort hatchback. "You're late," the nun shouted as she stood facing us in her long grey habit, her arms folded across her chest. When she demonstratively counted our vehicles one by one, pointing her finger at each vehicle in order, she demanded to know, "Where are the others?" I couldn't tell if she was joking or not so I looked to Barry, our team leader, and he said that "Sister Jo," as he called her, liked to talk tough but really wasn't. And she wasn't. As we exited our vehicles and started unloading she waved us in and told us there was plenty of fresh coffee and donuts in the kitchen.

Working with the kids was the best part of that day. It's not just that kids naturally want to help, though they do, but they want to show that they're good enough, that they're up to the task. They want your recognition and approval, but that's the same thing. I think it was the moment I had given one young girl a roller on a long pole and showed her how to apply the paint up and down a wall correctly that Thetis approached me from behind.

"Angel wouldn't even talk to anyone a week ago," I heard her say. I say "heard" because Thetis hadn't introduced herself yet and I didn't see her come up; I wasn't paying attention to anyone except the little girl. But I picked up on things right away.

"She's Angel?" I asked. "Is that her name or how you describe her?" We both stood admiring the little girl who seemed so earnest and focused.

"She's Angel," Thetis repeated. "Her brother is Domino. Don't ask."

We introduced ourselves and Thetis said it was nice that we would take time off to help the less fortunate. "You have to do it," I said. Thetis asked if I was aware of the crowded shopping malls and golf courses and any local tavern that was showing college football games on any given fall afternoon and I got her point.

Thetis had straight black hair like a Native American woman and with her tawny skin she looked a bit like Cher though I didn't make that association right away. Her features were sharp and appealing, intense but not zealous, and I loved her voice, too, a clarifying mezzo-soprano with perfect diction devoid of any affectation. I never looked at women's hands to see if they were married but I did then.

It was Thetis who got me started on a health kick. I always exercised, or just enough, and I was never overweight. But she was doing blood tests and cholesterol screening that day at the shelter and she asked me if I knew my blood type.

"Most people don't," she said, and I didn't. I didn't know what cholesterol was at all at the time either. She invited me into her little clinic behind a cotton drill screen in one of the classrooms and I loved how she unbuttoned the sleeve of my shirt and slowly rolled the cuff up my arm. I loved the way she slid her finger over my juicy vein, as she termed it.

I came back to the shelter every chance I could get that fall, sometimes collecting canned food on my own from the local Kroger or I'd buy a few cheap toys at Big Lots and sometimes I'd just bring an inflatable ball and take the kids of all ages out back to play kickball, a field game almost identical to what the English call rounders, which is the true origin of baseball. Thetis would come out and watch me when I'd do that and I remember the first time she took my arm in hers as we stood on the sidelines during a game. I wanted to kiss her then and there and I was sure she felt the same, and the main thing was we didn't have to say anything to each other, to explain or ask for permission, and I don't think either of us felt any embarrassment or shyness at all by that point. Years later I asked what she'd seen in me, seen first, that is.

"Well, you were a good-looking man when you were younger, Dwight," she said. "And you weren't narcissistic like other men. You never tried to show off."

WHEN IT was time to meet Judith Prime again I went downstairs and hopped into a cab for the two-mile trip from my hotel. I could have driven but one does not "hop into a cab" where I come from and so the act provided me with a splash of style and privilege I wasn't accustomed to. "Driver, Wally's on East Hubbard, and make it quick," I declared as I dropped down into the rear seat of a ten-year-old Ford

Crown Victoria. The Somali driver looked at me suspiciously in the rearview mirror and I explained that I was only joking, but I did ask him if he knew where it was.

"Yes, I know where it is," he said emphatically, almost defiantly, and he drove off.

Wally's Jazz Club is satisfyingly dark and intimate, with a small stage on the long side of the trapezoidal room and tables dispersed throughout like islands in an archipelago. I wonder what the venue felt like in days when the clubs like this featured sultry singers and sweaty fat dudes with lots of cash to throw at the suited maître d', long-legged cigarette girls whose bosoms bounced sublimely as they carried trays strapped to their necks. I easily conjure mobsters and local pols sitting in this or that corner inside Wally's, molls drooling over them, and private security guards always looking to the front door to see who it is that's just entered while those alluring females on stage with honeyed voices and plunging necklines covered the best in seventy-eight rpm records and made eyes at Big Daddy on cue. I imagine the real police outside the heavy doors telling gawkers to move along, and I imagine reporters with sweatbands on their felt fedoras and creases in their suits sitting at the bar pushing their shot glasses forward to be filled by a bartender who wore garters high up on each shirtsleeve and who had a long criminal record himself.

But it's not like that now. There are as many women as men in the club this evening, some sitting in their own conclaves, and the chatter is lively and the waiters scurry about with round metal trays held high on the palms of their hands, little martini glasses glinting off the crystal ceiling lamps, and I see my Judith seated at a small table back from the stage, which is occupied by a three-piece combo just setting up. I wave to her and walk over—she's dressed in a formfitting black dress made of a thin, shiny fabric and not much underneath.

"You must have closed that last sale," I say as I lean forward to give her a European-style kiss on the cheek, a gesture that surprises me but that she seems to take for granted. Prime tells me a client just accepted an offer on a condo in the Mies van der Rohe building on North Lake Shore Drive. She lifts her glass when she specifies that one and adds, "Six percent commission. It was my buyer too."

"Drinks are on you then," I tell her. She smiles.

"So what do you think?" Prime asks me as I sit across from her. "About the real estate market in general?"

"So what do I think about real estate opportunities in Chicago?" I repeat. "I think it's too easy to make money, is what I think. There must be a thousand people like me, or rather Bernie, who think they can make a killing here but, in truth, I don't see how that can really be. Either prices will be bid up too much or areas will be overbuilt or, I don't know, the kids will all move back in with their parents if the economy goes south again."

Prime carefully lifts her martini glass to her lips, then tips the glass into her mouth. Is she teasing me? "That's a very astute analysis," she says. "Only some people will hit the bull's-eye. Everyone else will fight for scraps at the margins or miss their targets altogether. That's why we continue to do research." Then she reaches for a file from the seat next to her and plops it on the table. "It's all in here," she says. "Ukrainian Village is the next big barn find, not Albany Park. That's where we want to go." She pats the top of the file with the palm of her hand and smiles triumphantly at me.

I sigh and tell her I'll take her word for it and add that I don't think I have an authentic investor's eye after all. It's just the parade of humanity, the famous divine comedy, that intrigues me, I say.

"And what will you tell Bernie?" she asks.

"To listen to you, not me."

"That's good."

We speak a little about culture in the city, about national politics, and Judith even asks what I like to do in my free time, what books I read and what movies I like to see. Judith is a good conversationalist but is it forced, like she's been seated next to someone she doesn't know at a wedding rehearsal and is compelled to talk to anyway? I, on the other hand, feel like I'm on a date. Forget the prostitute; this is a feeling I haven't had in a long time. I must be staring too intently into her eyes, leaning a bit too far forward over the table, and I suspect she senses the attention I'm paying to her. Is it flattering to her, or will she just humor me? Yet I know what I feel, and I'm as frightened as I am excited. Confused, as well. When did middle-aged women become so attractive? And why did Judith let me kiss her, if only on the cheek? She said earlier that she thinks I'm funny—that could have been a hint. The dress too. But maybe she thinks I'm just a silly old man and so I order myself to behave. The band soon begins a sound check and I turn my ears toward the stage; I wonder if they'll play "Autumn Leaves." I have the Roger Williams instrumental version at home, which was Thetis's and my favorite song.

CHAPTER 6

I keep Bertrand's old letters from the army, mostly from the time he first went away when it was still easy for him to write, in the top drawer of a narrow hall table near the front door in my house. I occasionally pull one out and read directly from it because there's just something about touching an actual piece of paper that someone else once touched, Michelangelo's *The Creation of Adam* in the real world. The letters are not holy, I know, yet lots of people save important words that have been impressed on parchment or paper like a sculptor's rasp or riffler on stone. The Jewish people, once they write something down in their holy books, they don't change it. The Jews are good about that. The Irish have long had the *Book of Kells* on display at Trinity College in Dublin, and then there are those Muslims who will threaten anyone who burns even a copy of the Koran. I had a teacher in high school who said he was friends with Aristotle, Tolstoy, Melville, and lots of other important thinkers and writers. "How can that be?" we students wanted to know. He said he spoke with them every evening in his capacious library, even visited them again and again when he was lonely. I think I'm closest to him. The letters from Bertrand are in my athenaeum.

"Dear Mom and Dad,

"Sorry I haven't written much. I've just been so busy lately (OK, everyone says that). But you wouldn't believe what I've been up to. (Actually, you really wouldn't believe it.) You'd think it's hot in Afghanistan but it got down to minus 5 or 6 last night. OK, that's Centigrade but try sleeping with only a simple bedroll and your field jacket to keep you warm. One of the guys had some home-baked cookies to eat (hint, hint, Mom) and they lasted, like, two hours. There's plenty of dust and gravel to go around if we want to make some stone soup, though.

"I don't want you to worry. I worry that you're worrying about me. Stop worrying! OK, it's nice to know that I have people back home who really care. I can't tell you how much that means to me. I know you only want what's best for me and that you always sacrificed for me. I don't want to disappoint you.

"Wait! A new shipment of cookies just came in. 'Be right there, Cal!' Gotta go.

"Love you, Mom and Dad. Bertrand."

Or should I read this one?

"Dad, this letter is for you. Mom — put it away if you're reading this.

"Dad—Did Grandpa or Great-Grandpa ever talk about killing someone? Recently we set up an ambush by a road that we knew the Taliban were using. It was a new moon, we had the high ground, and Zero Hour was near. It's not like five minutes to kickoff in a football game, Dad. No pacing, no chest thumps, no meditation. Well, maybe meditation. It was a lot like that Terrence Malick movie we saw, The Thin Red Line, I think. It was just quiet. A couple of guys prayed, but they don't like you to stare at them as they take a knee or make the sign of the cross. One of the deer hunters from Michigan, a good old boy from the Upper

Peninsula, had showed us how to build a blind in between some boulders and six of us held out for 30, maybe 36 hours, no campfires, no cigarettes, no phone traffic, not even a crapper, until finally we heard a small line of their pickups coming, then we saw the dust rising from the East. We knew they brought in supplies from Pakistan this way and when we could see them we saw that it was almost a convoy, eight pickups in all. We had our MANPATS and RPGs at the ready and we had enough ordnance but there were only six of us. The plan was to wait until they got past us and destroy them from behind and we had to be sure to fire all at the same time because they were going to fire back if they could, obviously. They all had machine guns mounted to the beds of their trucks, all Hilux Toyotas. When Hernandez gave the signal, we popped up from behind the rocks like prairie dogs and fired away. I think we hit three trucks immediately and you could see the men thrown from the backs or jumping from the cabs and some of the fighters did shoot back at us. I reached for a second MANPAT and hit another truck and took it out too. They were all destroyed in maybe 15 seconds but it seemed a lot longer, moment by moment always being more than seconds. But one of the Taliban was just standing between two burning truck carcasses, just standing there looking dazed, maybe 30 or 40 meters away and I could hear the crackling of the flames and ammo popping off and I could make out his face quite well and he just seemed confused, like he didn't understand why we had done this to him or even where he was. Ammo in the Toyotas continued to blow and the flames grew bigger and I could already feel the heat but none of us shot at him at first. He really was the last man standing so I picked up my M4, looked at him again and I think we made eye contact, and then I took him out.

"Bertrand."

In another letter, Bertrand announced that he'd met a girl overseas and I was reminded how young he still was and relieved that he could taste sweet normalcy in a time of war. He'd included a souvenir photo of himself and the girl standing on the Brighton Pier in the south of England. It was spring already in America but he and the girl were bundled up in pea coats with scarves tied around their necks, and I could tell from their body language that each was hunched up against a cold wind. In the background I could see the choppy waves in the water and on the pier itself I saw only a handful of people whose movements to and fro were arrested in time. Bertrand was smiling broadly but the girl's expression seemed a bit forced; she looked the chillier of the two so maybe that was it.

Bertrand wrote that the girl was a Canadian aid worker he'd met in Kabul who was on her way home after her year was up; he had two weeks of leave coming up so they decided to spend some time together before they went their separate ways, "nothing serious," he assured me.

In the letter he marveled at the working Gottlieb pinball games he'd discovered in an arcade on the pier—Sharpshooter, Barnacle Bill, even Ali-Baba, all with plenty of free plays and reverse flippers—as well as those "claw games," drop a coin in the slot and try to fetch a five-pound note from the bottom of the glass case. Bertrand and the girl had gone down by train for the day from London, where they were staying in a B&B in Bayswater. They'd caught *Sweeney Todd* at the Ambassadors Theatre, then dined in a restaurant with crystal light fixtures and bone-china plates, apparently it all made an impression on him. They did all the silly tourist things, too, Bertrand wrote—double-decker bus, Piccadilly Circus, and Hyde Park Speakers' Corner. "Some guy was arguing against the physical resurrection of Jesus," he wrote. "He stood on a box waving a picture of a corpse in rigor mortis and screamed, 'This is what you look like when you die.' The people surrounding him were just laughing, then he demanded to know how can the Son of God also be a God if there is only one God. I wanted to yell out, 'Cell division,' but then we just left."

They had a week left when the letter was sent off to me and Bertrand wrote that they were thinking of taking the train to Edinburgh or maybe a ferry to Dublin. "Have you ever been to Europe, Dad?" he asked, then answered his own question. "No, you don't travel much. It doesn't really matter, I suppose."

I didn't travel much? It was a subtle dig, which surprised me. When you're young you burst forth and do things, leap across a puddle when you're a child or climb a mountain when you're older and stronger, it all feels big, but then you settle into things. It's all part of a process, not failure, I wanted to say in my own defense. But I have at times found myself questioning my life's decisions, going over all the "what ifs," doing a postmortem of my life so far. Though I'd once justified my days selling encyclopedias as a rite of passage, my "gap year," I eventually wrote it off as lost time, even a form of mental illness from which I eventually recovered. But all that was wrong, I decided. If life is a series of experiences then that was one of them, no less valid than any other. It is only crass calculation that says every experience should aim toward a goal or end game, which usually is the bitch goddess success, I suppose. When I was younger I fretted over whether I'd be able to handle a nine-to-five job. Yet it was the nine-to-five regime that was the historical anomaly, a mere artifact of the industrial revolution. In human history, which is to say the evolution of the species, you marked time by the sun and did work *in season*, and a young man would have to go forth on his own, to go down in the valley and see what's there or run away to sea like Melville's men. Even selling encyclopedias when I was younger tested my manhood, at least that one time in Union City, a small town about ten miles south of Battle Creek, Michigan. I was traipsing up and down Division Street trying to sell my wares when I noticed smoke coming from a block farther down the way. This was a June or July day, I forget which, so I knew it wasn't someone burning leaves. Plus the smoke was fulsome, heavy and black. It had to be a house on fire. I carried my encyclopedias in a folding wire basket on wheels at the time but I abandoned everything and ran to the source of alarm.

It was indeed a house on fire. I found two women standing on the other side of the street, one yelling for someone to call the police, and a car coming from the opposite direction slowed, then stopped, and the driver peered out his window at the enveloping flames. No one acted, though, but I did. I ran up the broad steps to the home, a nice house with a wide veranda and a large dormer jutting out from the attic, and I opened the front door, which was unlocked. "Help," cried a woman in a simple sleeping gown; she stood at the foot of the stairs to the second floor. "My baby is up there!" Smoke was drafting down the stairs like billowing clouds; I could barely see my way clear to the landing but I didn't hesitate or ask further questions. "On the left," the woman cried. "The last door on the left."

And it was over quickly. The infant was in a playpen and she seemed almost to have been waiting for me because her arms clutched the top rail as she steadied herself, then she stretched a hand over the edge as she saw me bolt into the room. I think I just yanked that arm, maybe even knocked her against the side of the playpen before tucking her in more carefully into my body, her face against my chest, and I made my way cleanly down the steps and out onto the street.

The police, the volunteer fire department, and a local radio station reporter all arrived a few minutes later. No one died in the fire or even was seriously injured, but the house proved to be a total loss as the fire department's only pumper was hardly a weapon against the flames and the nearest fire hydrant was a block farther back, in front of the last house I'd stopped at to hawk encyclopedias. It took me some time to grasp the reality of it all though. I was a hero to the local townspeople: I had saved a child; I had acted heroically. "Weren't you afraid?" the radio man asked. He carried a portable tape recorder and microphone with him.

"I didn't have time to think," I told him. Then the reporter for the afternoon paper came by and he posed me for several pictures, one with my arm pointing to the burned-out corner of the remaining wall where I'd rescued the little girl, and another with my arm around the young mother, who'd been given a proper robe by a neighbor by that time.

As I lay in bed in my hotel room that night I decided to do a brief self-evaluation, a kind of exit interview in a mirror. I'd been brave enough, I told myself, but it wasn't much of a test. And it was only one test. I didn't want to exaggerate the significance of the day's events because, as I was to tell Bertrand many years later, you can lie to anyone else if you must but you never, ever lie to yourself.

Now it is time to tell you what I did for a living, that is, after I stopped selling encyclopedias to folks who lived well enough without them before I came knocking on their doors. Firstly, I did not go back to college. I was feeling a little old, more mature if not wiser, my adolescence over. I moved back in with Mom and Dad for a few weeks but only until I found a room through the classifieds with two guys who lived near the Eli Lilly and Company offices just south of downtown. One of the fellows, Hank, was a Vietnam veteran who worked security at Lilly and the other guy, Carleton, was a librarian at Indiana Central College which was a little farther south. Carleton was the landlord and we all lived in a small frame house with a great view of a new inter-state highway exchange. My roommates were not a rowdy pair, which was gratifying—no drunken tirades, no late-night police busts, not even many dirty dishes in the kitchen sink waiting for someone else to wash them. We'd have a back-yard barbecue in good weather and invite the neighbors over and if a couple of people had a guitar and a harmonica we'd have a hootenanny. I bought a used Dodge Dart with the reliable Slant-six motor, at least Dad said it was reliable, "not like those foreign jobs," he'd added. Hank, Carleton, and I sometimes would pile into it and drive to the Indiana State Fairgrounds where the Indiana Pacers played at the time—it was something else watching basketball in an arena where the cowboys also would rope steers and break broncos on the rodeo circuit. The Pacers played ball on hardwood, not sawdust and dirt though. My dad was later to complain when the Pacers left the fairgrounds for a new home, Market Square Arena, in 1974. "Build it or we'll move the team to another city," the owners had likely said. I looked up the original price of Market Square once, which was twenty-three million dollars. Even adjusted for inflation it was pennies on the dollar compared to what arenas go for today. It was torn down after twenty-five years, before it would have barely been old enough to qualify for historic license plates if it were a car, before it was barely older than a donkey's life expectancy, and replaced by a new arena that cost $183 million. I haven't bothered to adjust *that* price for inflation though.

Basically I enjoyed my time in "the shack," which is how Carleton, Hank, and I sometimes referred to our abode, and I stayed there for nearly three years. Soon the draft ended, and eventually the war, and it began to feel like a new era in America. I had a job, which was how I could pay rent and afford a car. I worked on the loading dock at L. S. Ayres— Mom had gotten me the job. Usually I'd just help people load furniture into the back of their Country Squire station wagons but sometimes management sent me out on appliance deliveries or, if the store was rearranging this or that department, they'd pull us all in to do the heavy lifting. My fellow workers often called me "College Boy," as in, "Hey, this ain't no job for a college boy to be doin', so why don't you sit there in the shade and a have a cool iced tea while we work our tails off," all said in jest, of course. Most of the guys I worked with, black or white, had never gone further than high school, if that, so a college dropout like me was a legitimate target. The job grew loathsome after a few months though—not just the bad managers checking up on us all the time, but a lot of the guys drank on the job and I'd taken up bumming cigarettes during breaks—plus I didn't want to see my mother *every* day, so I answered an ad in the paper for a driver at a NAPA auto parts store. I got to drive cars and pickups with large blue and yellow plastic baseball caps on the roofs but I also learned the difference between open and locking differentials, between camshafts and drive shafts, all of which had value to me.

Things in the shack got more interesting after Carleton's sister moved in. She just showed up one day—I first noticed the Renault Dauphine with California license plates parked in front—and I found her planting bulbs in the backyard. "Hi, can I help you?" I asked. It was just to start a conversation. I didn't know who she was at the time.

"They're gladioli and dahlias. I'm almost finished," she replied as she stood to face me. She'd been on her knees when I encountered her and she removed the green rubberized gloves she was wearing. "Hi, are you Dwight? I'm Cat, Carleton's sister." I think I said something stupid like, "I didn't know Carleton had a sister," and she said she'd just come back from San Francisco where she'd lived for a few years.

"I've never been there," I told her.

"No way," she exclaimed. "Fisherman's Wharf? The Embarcadero? *Haight-Ashbury?* Anyway, pleased to meet you."

I took a moment to behold her. She dressed the part, sort of—bell-bottom blue jeans, a knotty wool vest over an embroidered pale-yellow blouse, and a leather paddy cap covering her spiky blonde hair. Cat's face was highlighted by wide, thick brows that appeared to never have been plucked, which was fine, and her strawberry pink lips against her white flower-petal-soft skin was like a burst of April.

"What are you staring at?" she asked, tilting her head slightly to the side as she contemplated me too.

I didn't know what to say but I offered to help Cat as if I were a horticulturist myself, as if this was my garden or my passion. When she demurred, I told her to be sure to come inside for a drink when she was finished. "Is that your car out front?" I asked. The Renault Dauphine was sold in America for a few years in the early 1960s and I was amazed that it still ran, but more impressed that Cat wasn't driving a VW Beetle, which would have been so predictable otherwise. As I walked up the back steps to let myself into the house I turned and looked again at the girl who once more was on her knees pressing down on the brown earth with both hands. This was early spring, the trees were just starting to bud, and the air around me felt pure, not chilly, and the plentiful grey clouds

hanging low overhead were bracing, not threatening. I didn't
know at that moment that this young woman was moving in
with us but I felt that the needle had moved somehow. Cat
was not beautiful—different, certainly—and I had this strong
sensation that she'd always been there. I couldn't understand
how that could be but some people you meet you just feel
like you've always known them.

Carleton came home from the university about twenty
minutes later and went straight to the old Kelvinator refrigerator, grabbed a Meister Bräu beer, and pulled the ring tab.
"Want one?" he asked. The beer foamed from the top and
over his hand as he spoke. I told him I'd already had one.

"I figure you've met Cat," he continued. "She's going to
live with us for a while."

By the early 1970s almost no one spoke of hippies anymore. Haight-Ashbury was passé, young men at elite universities had figured out how to beat the military draft even
before it was abolished, and the sexual revolution had claimed
total victory. Even abortions were legal, albeit still controver-
sial. Cat had indeed come from San Francisco where she'd
lived since she ran away from home in 1967, I learned. I
imagined her time of druggies, free love, and annoying Hare
Krishna acolytes; I imagined colored glass beads around her
neck and flowers in her hair and underground poets, too, or
was that all in some dumb *Time* magazine article I'd once
read? Cat turned out to be none of the above and all the
above—she would not talk about her days there or share
any artifacts, which in itself was highly suggestive, but as
a member of the house she was an All-American girl, part
tomboy and part Girl Scout, one of the guys and Tinker Bell
too. I learned that both she and Carleton had grown up on
a farm in northeastern Indiana as members of a strict Men-
nonite sect, so maybe that explained why one child found

refuge in books while the other had found life in an alternate universe altogether.

THOUGH *The Drew Carey Show*, which was set in Cleveland, was not to appear for more than twenty years, I can say that life in the shack anticipated events pretty well. Maybe *Friends* too. We'd all go bowling or out for a couple of drinks together, preferably at working-class bars near the old Chrysler foundry or one of the meat-packing plants still operating in the city, and Hank would take us to his American Legion Post on occasion, which in fact is where Cat got her first job once back in Indiana. Hank arranged that.

Post Eighteen was a dark, smoky place filled with heavily shellacked pine furniture, bingo on Tuesday nights, and poker games in a back room anytime they could get up enough hands. Bartenders knew all the regulars, the burly old sergeants and emphysemic privates alike, men who'd flirt with waitresses and pinch their bottoms even if their wives were in tow. The older waitresses—most were older— always called their customers Sugar or Honey, sometimes endearingly Young Man, if the veteran already was totally grey-haired and parked a cane at the side of his table. Tips were uneven—"I gave at Bien Hoa," or "I gave on Omaha Beach," some would say—but others would drop a twenty-dollar bill easily into the palm of a waitress and squeeze her hand hard, a legacy more than a tip as they knew they could outlast their fallen comrades only so much longer. Cat apparently was one of the more popular waitresses and she liked to tell us stories after a shift.

"I can't imagine what it was like," she'd once said to a veteran. "You could have been killed at any time." Cat

said the men at the table all laughed at her, but not mali-
ciously so.

"And what did you do for 'R and R,'" Cat said she'd
once asked another former soldier. "I hear it got pretty wild
in Saigon. You see any action there?"

"Yeah, what was that madame called?" another soldier
nearby had interjected. "You came runnin' down the stairs
at that whore house pretty quick. What happened, Keith?"

It was that kind of talk all the time at Post Eighteen, Cat
said.

Carleton was the old guy in the house at thirty-two, mild-
mannered and very disciplined in his personal habits whether
that was keeping his shelf in the refrigerator well-stocked and
ordered or jogging several times a week in all but the worst
weather. I'd occasionally run with him and he always set a
good pace. It was the farm experience, I concluded, and I
asked him once which he liked better, the farm or the city.
He mulled my question, then impressed me with a nuanced
reply.

"It's not that I'm against animal husbandry or the cycli-
cal nature of planting in the spring and harvesting in the fall,
not at all. But I like books more. When I was younger I'd
thought of becoming a monk and transcribing all the great
books, religious and secular, by hand. Now I get to research
interesting questions. It's good. I like the accumulation of
knowledge even more than the growth of the soil."

Hank never was the talkative one, not about Vietnam,
not about his background or family back home, wherever
that might be, and not about his job working security for
Lilly, except when he'd occasionally mock "all those limos"
the bigwigs rode in or he'd be talking about the numbers
game the limo drivers helped run. Once he told us about a
janitor who tried to walk out of the building with a gross of

Ceclor, which was a serious antibiotic. "How in the world do you fence antibiotics?" Hank asked incredulously one evening. "Maybe sleeping pills or birth control pills. But antibiotics? Maybe he was going to sell it to the Cubans." Hank was a good-looking guy, sandy-haired like a California surfer, toothy as a rabbit, and seemingly uncomplicated. He rode a Harley-Davidson Sportster in his time off, one with a peanut gas tank and valanced steel fenders, and he gave us all rides one day, which Cat found exhilarating. Soon she and Hank were going on long rides together, then playing footsie with each other as we all watched *The Tonight Show starring Johnny Carson* in the living room, then they were coming down for breakfast together. Things became official, so to speak, when Cat announced she was moving into Hank's room full-time. Forget the *Friends* TV show reference. There must be Harlequin Contemporary Romances where these things happen, friends and lovers living in the same house, everyone with their own secrets, but biding time too.

I must admit I wasn't indifferent about Cat. Maybe it was the closeness—sometimes we'd pass in the hall in the middle of the night coming or going to the toilet and she'd be wearing only panties but would fold her arms across her breasts and smile shyly at me but say nothing of it the next day. I remember thinking once that she was a little plump, but not overly so. I figured that's how farm girls were.

Though Hank diligently went to work every day and continued to ride his motorcycle, or work on it as needed, he became more withdrawn over time, not wanting to go out as part of the group anymore or even with Cat much. One evening she asked what I thought was going on with him.

"Seriously," she said, leaning forward on the plush sofa we had in the living room. Cat never wore a bra and I kept my eyes up. "Do you think it's the war? He's badly scarred, you know."

"You mean psychologically." I was seated in a wicker peacock chair that Cat had recently purchased. She wagged a finger at me.

"No, I mean he has actual scars on his back and side. He says he got them in hand-to-hand combat with Charlie, you know, the Viet Cong. Haven't you ever seen Hank naked?"

It was an odd question, I thought at the time. "I don't shower with him," I said and I immediately regretted my comment. Cat would see it as a dig or worse, a reflection of my jealousy. "Most vets, they don't want to talk about it," I said after recovering. "My dad, he won't talk about World War II much. He enlisted in the Canadian Armed Forces in 1940, you know."

What an odd thing for me to bring up, I immediately thought after I spoke those words. I knew what it meant too. I was being defensive. I didn't want this young woman to think less of me just because I hadn't been a warrior like her boyfriend. I almost brought up Carleton's case—*And how did he beat the draft?*—but what would that have to do with Cat? My reference to the Canadian Army had piqued Cat's interest though.

"Your dad did that?" she asked. "That's so cool. Did he fight the Germans?"

Well, Cat was no intellectual and I tried not to be too proud. After all, it was my dad who'd joined the fray, not me. In any case, we returned to Hank. It transpired that he was having nightmares, not that he'd discuss them, but Cat knew something was going on inside his head because he'd sit up suddenly in bed in the middle of the night and look around, demand to know who was out there, even call out to his buddies to get their guns. Cat said she'd put his head against her bosom and gently rock him while she tousled his hair.

"I try to make love to him at those times just to get his mind off things but he can't," she said. "It's not that he's impotent, believe me, but he's so shaken."

In the coming days and weeks, I looked for signs of deterioration in Hank's demeanor. I'd joined a scratch basketball team at the YMCA and I invited him to come along one evening but he declined. A fellow at the NAPA store was thinking of purchasing a secondhand Triumph motorcycle; could Hank help us check it out? Even that didn't engage him.

"Cat's been talking about me, hasn't she," he finally said.

I was going to bullshit him but decided not to. It was an early Saturday morning and Cat was working a pancake breakfast at the American Legion Post and I was about two hours away from having to start my shift at the auto parts store. Carleton had made a rare visit to the family homestead in northeastern Indiana for the weekend. Hank and I were huddled under our separate blankets on the back porch at the time; frost had formed on the grass overnight and glistened keenly under the rising sun.

"Yeah, she's told me a little," I said. "She's worried. She cares about you."

"No, she doesn't, Dwight," he replied. "People only care about themselves."

"Well, you've been to war. Everybody wants to survive. That's not the same thing."

He looked at me and harrumphed. "Like you know, right," he said.

Hank committed suicide two weeks later. The autopsy revealed that he'd taken a lethal mix of alcohol and barbiturates, which was more of a Hollywood way of doing it than a guy who'd blown out a few people's brains at five hundred meters, but that's what he did. The shitty thing was that he drank his toxic potion before going to bed with Cat—he must have hidden in the kitchen, or in a corner, while mixing the ingredients, methodically and surreptitiously committing himself to his personal extinction—and then he calmly climbed into bed with an unsuspecting girlfriend. When Cat woke up early the next morning and touched his very cool body at her side, she understood immediately, she said. She felt guilty at first that she hadn't anticipated his actions, hadn't done more, but I told her that she had done what she could. "You can influence events but you cannot determine them," I said. I thought what Hank had done, letting her be the one to discover his corpse, leaving her the nightmare memory of having lain next to his stiffening body for hours after he'd died, was very cruel. It was exactly that, but maybe that was the lesson he wanted to teach her. The world was a cruel place.

Cat began to open up to me after Hank's death, slowly at first, but in the end like a carnation bloom. She said religion never bothered her, it was all theater to her, and she couldn't have had a happier childhood growing up on the farm. She'd looked forward to her chores every morning and if it was cold she'd eagerly don her tights, vest, and canvas chore coat, heavy wool hunting socks, and high rubber boots, too, and go milk the cows and feed the chickens. In summer she loved dripping with sweat as she weeded soybean fields or detasseled corn, besting most of the boys she worked with too. "Do you know how to tell the difference between corn and beans?" she asked me, teased me, basically. I told her I didn't. "Well, you know what stalks of corn look like, right?" I told her I did. "Well, if it ain't corn then it's beans." She laughed uproariously after she told me that, as if it was the funniest thing in the world. I couldn't contain my laughter, either, although of course I knew the difference between corn and beans. Everyone in Indiana knows that. I didn't let on though. I wasn't about to break the mood. I just leaned forward and kissed her for the first time.

Cat did not immediately want to have sex with me and I understood—it was Hank. She'd already changed jobs because of him, saying she didn't want to keep talking to men at the American Legion Post about how sad it was, how hard civilian life can be on soldiers, or just having to nod and sigh every time someone offered their condolences. Cat had taken a job at a major landscaping firm and would come home with dirt on her face and under her fingernails and her clothes would be soiled, even greasy; she looked like something pulled out of the rich soil herself, and she'd bound upstairs to take a shower and come out renewed, fresh, glowing.

I was surprised when Cat and I finally hooked up. It was several weeks after the funeral and late one evening I heard a tapping on my door. "Come in," I said. I didn't know for sure it would be Cat but maybe I dreamed it would happen this way. I sat up in my bed and saw her standing in the doorway backlit by a small sconce down the hall, then she slowly pulled her T-shirt over her head.

"I don't like being alone," she said as she climbed into bed next to me, "but I guess you've figured that out by now."

Life changed very little in the shack once Cat moved in with me. Carleton now had two empty bedrooms he could rent but chose not to do so, which made me feel more Harlequin Gothic than Contemporary Romance, especially as Cat started dressing more skimpily while at home. "Well, it's just you and my brother," she rebuked me when I raised the issue with her one time.

"Exactly," I said.

I do remember one evening very well. There was to be an open house at the Butler University observatory and Cat asked if I wanted to see the stars with her. "You don't have to be a student or a professional astronomer," she said. "It'll be just like Natalie Wood and James Dean."

I didn't immediately get the movie reference but I hadn't visited that observatory since I was a child.

"I checked the weather in the paper. Clear night and it's a new moon," she said.

"I'd love to," I told her. "Is Carleton coming along?"

"Naw," she said. "He'd just be Sal Mineo. Besides he has to work tonight."

Once there we had to wait in line for twenty minutes, then move along, but we could look through the telescope and I felt I was peering deeper into the vacuum of space than I had on any dark night on my own. The sky had shades of blackness to it like ancient tombs and was more layered than even a poem. Cat later noted how people often say they feel small and unimportant after experiencing the universe like this but that she felt empowered just because she was a part of such grandeur.

I took Cat to visit my parents on occasion, Sunday afternoon dinners, Mom's birthday, things like that. She never dressed up for the visits, arguing that it would be dishonest. I don't think Mom liked her very much; Cat was strange fruit I must have plucked from some invasive tree. My mother was very much of the Mamie Eisenhower generation, always proper, a Loretta Young clone. I hadn't known who Loretta Young was before Mom started watching her on TV in the 1950s; Mom loved the showy, glamorous entrance the svelte performer would make at the start of her shows, doing a three-hundred-sixty-degree spin after walking through tall french doors into an exquisite ballroom or dramatically opening a door in a swank Manhattan apartment with a swoosh that was palpable in your own living room, always while wearing the latest fashions from *Vogue* magazine. Cat was Annie Oakley go get a gun, she was a Soviet hero driving her own tractor across Ukrainian wheat fields. She was no Loretta Young.

Dad pulled me aside one time and asked me if I was serious about "this girl," which told me he wasn't taken with her either. But it made me think. Was I serious about Cat or had I just fallen for her unconventional charms? Couples are meant to get married, have children, and then stay home and watch programs like *The Loretta Young Show* together. That was life according to Robert Young, the Reverend Billy Graham, and Mom and Dad. Or if I was a farmer I'd be expected to work the forty acres when the time came or take over the family business if father had been a haberdasher or a printer or an independent Rexall pharmacist. Sure, I was comfortable with Cat and even relieved not having to be on the prowl every night yet I was beginning to feel pulled apart. Basically Dad's question had shined a light far into a future yet unfulfilled.

Cat and I eventually moved out of Carleton's house and into an older high-rise apartment in a once fashionable but now tired neighborhood in Indianapolis. We liked its tile-lined vestibule and real brass elevator, the high ceilings and hardwood floors in all the rental units too. Most of our neighbors were widows and widowers who had lived there for decades, who still dressed in jacket and tie if they were men and short heels and full dresses if they were women even if they weren't going anywhere and hadn't left the building for days. We'd committed to moving there before realizing that neither of us had much furniture of our own so we slept the first few nights in sleeping bags and ate breakfast at a local pancake house down the street, dinner at a Mexican restaurant up the street. I rented a truck and we picked up some items at Goodwill, the usual table and chairs, yet another cheap, floral print sofa, and odd lots of dishes and cutlery. We bought a new mattress and had it delivered, and Cat had saved her wicker peacock chair. I could have borrowed a few items from my parents but I didn't tell them what I was up to right away. I quit my job at NAPA too. It felt like I was starting over all over again and I wasn't really going to deliver auto parts for the rest of my life, was I? In the first few weeks of our newfound freedom Cat and I would smoke weed, which she had no trouble sourcing, and we looked at lots of travel brochures to the most unlikely places such as Trinidad in the Caribbean, the northern Yukon, and how to win free land somewhere in the arid regions of Western Australia.

Mom and Dad became concerned when they tried to reach me at Carleton's and he told them I'd moved out and had left no forwarding address. That actually was not true. He knew exactly where we were but I guess he didn't want to get in the middle of things. Cat and I hadn't applied to Ma Bell for a phone—that part was true—as there was a pay phone down the hall on every floor and a wooden phone booth with glass panels in the lobby. There was a front desk where one could leave messages, of course, and I should have given the building's phone number to my parents sooner.

Cat and I stayed together for a further eight months and she turned out to be a wild horse that I couldn't break. I had dreams for the future. Everyone has dreams. But for Cat it was more like she was living the fantasy right now. After about a month in the new apartment I'd gotten another job, this time at Galyan's Trading Company, which was a local sporting goods company before it was sold to the Dick's Sporting Goods chain. If nothing else I figured I'd learn about golf clubs or ski shoes or skeet shooting, plus they had a pension plan, something Dad had always touted as a worker's right. I don't want to say that familiarity breeds contempt but you do discover other people's bad habits. Though Cat knew how to cook she started serving odd meals when it was her turn to make dinner. Some nights we'd have boiled potatoes, but only boiled potatoes. Or we'd have a chicken, literally, one whole chicken baked in the oven, then dropped onto a white ceramic serving dish in the middle of the table. Or a bag of carrots or a bowl of apples. Every meal was one or two items only. I asked her if it was too hard to prepare a more complex meal but that only led to a fight. After a while I dug out a recipe for meat loaf and made several pans or I'd bring meals home in a sack from one fast-food place or another. I also boiled a dozen eggs at a time which sufficed for breakfast for a week when paired with wheat toast and Cheerios.

The best thing about life with Cat was the sex. She was voracious to the point of being addicted. She even began telling me about her other lovers save Hank. Not just outlandish tales of doing it on a mountaintop or in an abandoned barn, but even playing spin the bottle at a party and everybody hooked up with someone new. I saw that she had a black widow's way of seducing men, targeting them and drawing them in. "You should write a book," I told her.

"I am," she said.

We were on the floor in the living room that night and we could hear the slap of car tires on the rainy pavement below and hear the occasional bang and clank of the apartment's cast iron steam heat registers, even see the diffuse lights from the city pasted onto the cloud cover above. I felt as if we were on a tramp steamer traveling somewhere distant and forbidden but it would be exciting once we got there. I asked Cat if I was in her book. "You will be," she said.

It really had taken me too long before I understood that Cat came under the heading of "free spirit." I saw that, for her, freedom meant no responsibilities, no commitments, no life other than the present. Had I fallen into a trap, even one of my own making? Cat had taken a new job, albeit part-time, working banquets for a well-known caterer that serviced all the downtown hotels. I would tell her how cute she looked in the black trousers, red sash, and starched white shirt that made up her uniform, even help her with the mandatory black satin bow tie, and I'd wait for her to come home after any late-night affair. Then one time she didn't come home after hosting a bachelor party and I stayed up all night waiting for her. When she finally turned up she had that guilty but deeply contented look on her face, that walk-of-shame cadence as she stepped through the door of the apartment and I knew right away what had happened. "Was it the best man or one of the groomsmen?" I asked.

"Oh, I don't know," she said. "Maybe it was the groom himself. You know, one last bash before his period of confinement."

The next day Cat said she was moving out. "It's been fun," she told me. "A real gas. Isn't that what kids say? I'll pay my share of the rent and utilities for the month, of course."

I wasn't broken up over Cat. We were on a month-to-month lease, maybe with each other as well, and I moved out of the apartment shortly after she did. I moved in with a guy who managed the fishing lines and lures at Galyan's and I donated most of my furniture and bric-a-brac back to Goodwill. I returned to my parents' good graces, which is not to say they'd ever abandoned me, but they'd known enough to stay a safe distance back, a lesson I never forgot. In any case, Cat had been a learning experience for me. It made me appreciate Thetis even more when I met her. You see, you don't marry your girlfriend. You marry your wife.

CHAPTER 7

I look at the towering cottonwood tree behind my house, its trunk thick and straight as an oak, and I say to myself, "Why does no one make a table or chair from a cottonwood tree?"

"You should cut that thing down. It could fall on your roof," my neighbor had advised me. I understood—it was the violent storms we often have in Indiana—so I obtained a quote to have it done. Not from the illegals I've seen working in the neighborhood, you can tell who they are by their unmarked vans and how they look away when you first notice them, but I'd rather support the good ole boys who've been cutting trees and nailing roof tiles and rolling their own cigarettes in Indianapolis since they came north in the 1930s and '40s, that other great migration after all the agricultural jobs moved to California. Today is the day they've come with their bucket truck and log loader.

"That's some big ass tree," Billy says to me. Billy is the ginger-haired scion of Taylor's Tree Removal and he's dressed in Lee denim overalls—the garment is suspended from his shoulders like vestments—and his mud-encrusted Chippewa boots have a "Made in America" tag at each tongue.

"What do you do with the wood once you haul it off?" I ask Billy. We're standing under the sun in my backyard;

it's high noon and the tree towers over us like a three-stage rocket.

Billy spits from his mouth, then packs in more chew between his lower lip and gum. "Pallets," he says, then he waits for me to tell him what I want to do. He's quoted me twelve hundred dollars for the job and I think that is a high price to pay to remove a tree, but what's a cottonwood good for anyway?

It's going to be a long afternoon so I go down to the liquor store while the boys commence work. "Where do you keep the Scotch whiskey?" I ask.

"Same place as last week," the clerk replies. She's a middle-aged woman with frazzled bleached-blonde hair and skin that's cracked and browned like breaded pork chops, like she smokes too much, and I smile but don't get mouthy with her because it's just a little game we play with each other. I usually buy Johnny Walker Red or J&B Rare but the clerk tells me they have Grant's on special this week.

As long as you're up get me a Grant's. That's the line in a magazine ad I remember from my youth. I was enthralled when the latest issue of *Life* would arrive in the mail each week and I'd look at the ads first, what rich people could buy, or so I thought at the time. A man sits in a leather hammock chair with chrome rails, very mid-century modern they'd call it today, and he leans on his elbow on the armrest and says to someone off-camera, "As long as you're up get me a Grant's." It had to be a woman, she must have been beautiful and obedient, which was all a man wanted in 1958.

In 1958.

Once back home I check the mail, it's utility bills and two-for-one coupons at Arby's and a solicitation from the World Wildlife Fund, and I drop down into my easy chair and twist open the cap on my bottle of Grant's. A glass tumbler from the previous night is at my side and as I fill it and hold the glass to my lips I listen to the sound of chain saws ripping through the wind outside, the crunch and thud of another limb landing on the hard ground just outside my field of vision, and I sigh.

I DIDN'T think I'd miss my cottonwood but its absence has changed my mornings. I'd never had trouble sleeping before but without that big tree to intercept the morning sun when it comes over the neighboring rooftops, it feels like a search-light has been aimed at me. The only defenses left to me are a hawthorn, but it's low to the ground and not much denser than a crab apple tree; a blue beech that I like very much, but it's as thin and wiry as an ironwood tree and no thicker at the base; and a flowering dogwood that only delights for a few days in the spring. I could close the shades at bedtime but I won't do it because I like the sense of a blue velvet sky swaddling the world at night and the twinkling lights from a small airplane heading somewhere, and especially great big moons when they rise just after dark. I can't close the shades. But the big tree is gone and the birds that nested there are gone too. Have they migrated, or were they evicted? Jays and cardinals and shrikes, birds that chirp and some that caw. Sometimes I would lie in bed of a morning and listen to them, but now they've become scarce. I did this.

I roll over to the edge of my bed and sit up, the stiffness draining slowly from my body like lactic acid after a workout, and only then do I stand and stretch. After peeing I wash my hands and don my robe, then I go downstairs to fix break-fast. It's a very perfunctory thing for me to do since Thetis died—it will always be two scrambled eggs and a Thomas brand English muffin, orange juice ("fresh squeezed, never frozen," the bottle says but it's still not the same as squeezing the oranges myself), and a bowl of cereal afterward, usually Bran Flakes or Special K with 1 percent milk. Breakfast with Thetis was different—omelets with diced onions and green peppers or healthy Irish oatmeal with raisins or even a half cantaloupe with light whipped cream if we were dieting. Sometimes she and Bertrand would make breakfast together, that is, when he was younger. He especially liked to beat the eggs in a stainless-steel bowl we had, then carefully flip the omelet in an iron skillet we always used. It's not that I didn't cook back then; on occasion I would volunteer to make breakfast for the family, dinner too, but only on occasion. I liked the sound of something sizzling on a griddle as much as anyone, the smell of fresh bread in the oven, even the buzzer going off after a slow roast was done.

On this day, however, I hurry through breakfast because I have somewhere new to go. I've signed up to work as a judge for the next general election and I have to attend a training session; all the volunteers are to meet at the Hamilton County Courthouse in Noblesville at ten A.M. It's about eight miles from where I live and I decide to ride my bicycle, not to be eccentric or because I think I belong in an AARP commercial, but I want to be true to who I am. I map out the route in my head, deciding to stay close to the curb even if that means risking flats from all the debris strewn there, and I'll wear my yellow reflective vest just in case. It's a cool morning and I decide to put on an old pair of chinos with a big rubber band to tie around my right leg.

I've read up on our historic county courthouse. Like so many other early civic buildings in America it was meant to symbolize something, in this case authority as well as inspire awe, a secular temple of the New Rome. The architecture all is derivative, of course, but at least not neo-Classical in this instance. Second Empire, actually, after the French, with mansard roofs, lots of ornamentation and four-square symmetry surrounding a central dome. The building must have been quite a sight on the banks of the White River when it opened in 1879—I wonder what the nearby Miami and Delaware Indians thought of it then. I make it to my landmark in about thirty-five minutes.

The training takes place in a high-ceilinged room in one wing that thankfully hasn't been modernized, meaning no fluorescent tube lighting, no fabric-covered institutional seating, no Dalton, Georgia, carpeting by the yard. I appreciate the heavy oak chairs with turned armrests, the narrow plank maple floors, even the roller shades in the tall windows. The hollow sounds bouncing off the original lath-and-plaster walls too. There are about thirty of us present to receive training and most people appear to be retirees like myself. I sit next to a woman who introduces herself as Martha and she asks if I'm new. The question surprises me because it is a training session, after all, and I think she sees a certain dubiousness on my face. "I repeat my training every two years," she quickly adds. "The vote is a very sacred right, you know."

I nod in agreement. "Yes, we have to ensure that every vote counts," I say. I think she's quite sincere and it's the least I can do to be amicable. The woman is not finished though.

"What if a ballot is spoiled? Or someone has come to the wrong place and needs help finding their precinct? And there's always problems with write-ins." The woman sighs, and then she pulls a quart-size bottle of Gatorade from a shopping bag at her side and chugs it heartily. When she's finished she smacks her lips and returns the bottle to the bag, then she folds her hands across her lap and looks straight ahead. In a few moments the county clerk walks in—I recognize her from the campaign ads and posters during the last election—and she waves and smiles to several people in attendance and I sense that there is a bit of clubby atmosphere in the room. An assistant follows and passes packs of notes down every row; when I receive mine, I see that it's at least one hundred pages of mostly screenshots from a Power Point demonstration.

There are questions from the audience as we go along— "What if a voter has left her ID at home? Do they have to declare their party affiliation in a general election like they do in a primary?"—and I know it's all important stuff, but I can't help looking at the clock.

The county clerk gives us some additional information such as, for example, we're not allowed to leave the polling place at all. I think to myself that they're afraid we might not come back but it's really about the independence of the poll workers and the chain of custody for the ballots. I also learn that lunch will be provided or we can bring our own and receive a twenty-dollar allowance. I'll take the Andrew Jackson, please, as if pizza slices and a can of Pepsi could be worth twenty dollars. Martha catches me snickering about all this and I wonder if she's going to turn me in. The session seems interminably long but when the clerk asks if there are any more questions and no one raises a hand applause breaks out across the room, so I know everyone is good-natured about things. And it's only eleven forty-five A.M. when we're dismissed—not so bad after all. I can hop on my bike and go home, maybe make a side trip along rural roads in the county, or I can stay in town for lunch. It's been awhile since I've explored a classic courthouse square in Indiana, which is as iconic as Grant Wood's *American Gothic.*

In the Rust Belt a lot of small town squares look the same—a tanning salon, an antique store, a restaurant that's little more than a lunch counter with a few gingham-covered tables on an old linoleum floor, maybe a health department outreach program, just lower-tier businesses and enterprises like that. Lots of spaces for rent too. But if it's a county seat then things will be better. Law offices will abound and there may be enough money in circulation to support a jewelry store, a women's fashion boutique, a nice tavern or two, and real restaurants, the kind that have a full menu and stay open at night. Noblesville has all that plus a little ice cream shop, an insurance agency, even an old time hardware store with a cowbell that rings when you open the front door and shelving in back you can pick from yourself. The single screen movie theater is long gone but you still get a feel of how things were when the farmers would come to town on a Saturday afternoon and stay awhile. I'm hungry enough after my earlier ride and then the training session and I decide to stop into Famous Smiley's, A Tradition Since 1946, for lunch. I lean my bike against a lamppost and wrap my cable lock around it—I feel like I'm hitching a horse in the Old West—and I enter. Famous Smiley's is a cozy place—there's a hand-rubbed wood bar on one side of a narrow aisle and booths on the other side with space for a coin-operated pool table under a tin shade in back before you get to the kitchen, which features a swinging door with a small porthole window. I sit at the bar.

"How ya' doin'?" the barkeep asks as he wipes down the counter in front of me with a small towel he's pulled from his shoulder; it's just like a scene from a noir fifties film. "What can I get ya?"

The man is middle-aged, has a bad comb-over, and is just this side of portly. His pockmarked face tells me he had bad acne as a kid that was left untreated. I want to ask how long he's tended bar, what's it like to have an old-fashioned job like that in an old-fashioned bar like this. It would be condescending on my part, yet I often wonder how people spend their lives, how they end up where they are, and what accommodations they've had to make along the way. I just don't see bartending as aspirational anymore. I'm sure it's how he has supported himself his whole life and what he'll be remembered for when he dies.

Shit, I say to myself. I don't know any of this to be true. I don't know the man at all. Why do I worry about what other people are really like?

The man is very patient; he leans with both his hands on the inside rail and waits for me to order. "What do you have on tap?" I ask.

He points to a series of nearby handles, all of which have clear logos on them, and starts by saying, "Well, let's see. We've got Miller and Miller Lite on tap, then there's Heineken, some German imports and a couple of local craft brews, and some other brews in bottles." I'm chagrined. I think he's playing me a bit because of course I can read and there's a card in a holder in front of me with all the beers listed anyway.

"I'll take one of the craft beers, whatever you recommend," I say, then I quickly amend my statement. "No. Miller is fine. Why change now?"

The man asks if I want anything to eat and I look up at the menu board high above the back bar. Prices are reasonable. I ask if the ocean perch is fresh or frozen and he just smiles. "OK, I'll take a hamburger then," I say. "No. Make it a cheeseburger and heavy on the tomato. And fries, but a small basket, if you have that." He sort of slaps a hand on the counter and walks off with my order.

I enjoy the knock and crack of pool balls being struck in the distance, the jabber from men talking to each other, sometimes raucously but not in anger, and I like the subdued lighting that allows the neon beer signs to glow even more iridescently. I turn and look around at the wall hangings and I see something that appears to be a yellowed newspaper clipping so I decide to walk over and read it. I just know it's going to be the story behind Famous Smiley's.

"With his separation pay, Staff Sgt. William 'Smiley' Jones signed a deal in 1953 with a liquor distributor and rented space on the Noblesville Courthouse Square in what has since become an Indiana tradition . . . ." The article continues that Jones was from Indianapolis, served as a warehouseman in San Diego and Honolulu during the Korean War, and was the first black man to own a business in Noblesville.

"Smiley died in '86," the bartender says from behind. "A couple of lawyers own the place now."

I return to the bar to find my food served. "How long have you worked here?" I ask.

"Since May," he answers. "When the stone quarry closed I decided I wasn't going to do nasty work anymore. How's the beer?"

THETIS LIKED to stop into antique stores. A lot of our furniture over the years came from such places but only solid wood pieces. She didn't want the smoke and sweat and stink of other people's bodies in any fabric-covered things we might purchase and she always said reupholstering is a lost art. My favorite piece, which I still have, is an oak library table with four-inch square legs and a double-thick top. There's a cigarette burn near one edge but I like the image it conjures of a lean man in a coarse wool suit who's bent over the stock quotations or perhaps the ship arrivals in the local paper while smoking his "tailor-mades." There's an antique store on the courthouse square and I decide to stop in. I first see the displays of toy cars and small tin soldiers and baseball cards, very common fare, then a display of lampshades with knotted fringes and ceramic bowls of blue and a woman under a floppy felt hat comes up to me and asks if she can help and I say that I'm just looking and she says if I should need any help just ask and I thank her and I do walk to the back of the store where the heavier items are located. There's an old pine wardrobe with doors that are no longer square that's priced at $1,250 and a ceramic-coated gas stove with chromed brass fixtures that is nice but it's $2,495 and carries a caveat to see a professional before installation—and just for a moment, she passes before my eyes like a wind-blown leaf, I see Thetis and she tells me that we don't need anything here, maybe some other time, let's move on. Truly, it never takes much to bring Thetis to mind again either.

I remember a short trip Thetis and I once made to New Harmony, deep in the southwest corner of the state, which had recently been touted by a national travel magazine as one of the "ten best" hidden treasures in America and "the crown jewel of Indiana tourism." Thetis had wanted to visit the Historic District, site of not one but two attempts at Uto-pian societies in the early nineteenth century. We finally went on a crisp Saturday morning in mid-October, which is always my favorite time of year. I remember the dry yellow leaves kicked up in the air as we roared down the back roads, win-dows rolled down because I wanted to hear the rush of wind, feel its bite, and Thetis wrapped her arms around her chest to fight the chill but did not complain. It takes three hours to reach New Harmony if traveling directly from Indianapolis, short enough to feel like a lark, long enough to feel like a journey. The original dwarf village was founded in 1814 by the Harmonie Society, a group of Pietists who'd fled their native Germany to settle in Pennsylvania and then decided to move even farther from sin; they settled on twenty thousand acres of swampland near the Wabash River in southwestern Indiana where they built log cabins and small brick buildings, many of which still stood when we visited, while they worked to drain the swamps and grow crops. No matter though—half the people died of malaria anyway so they moved yet again, to the four winds this time. The settlement sat abandoned only for a short while; a man named Robert Owen and a few friends from their native Wales bought the property in 1824 and tried their hands at utopia too. Owen was as much a radical social reformer as a Christian—he opposed the institution of marriage and the existence of private property, among other things. I was all for visiting New Harmony because I liked the architecture that I'd read about there, from the original log cabins all in neat rows like barracks to the Working Men's Institute, a brick edifice built after the Owens people had gone, too, but not their influence. About one thousand people lived in the new part of town when we visited; tourism was the big industry.

A handful of other visitors nodded politely as we passed them on the dirt roads of the original settlement. "To think, I could have washed linen all day, or mopped the floors and darned socks and cooked the stew in cast iron pots over a hearth," Thetis observed at one point. "Would the men have hunted, or worked in the fields?"

"Probably pray," I said, then quickly corrected myself. "That was unfair. This was a working community. You were self-sufficient just because nobody owed you anything, including God."

Thetis turned to me and put her hand to my chest. "So you do know about the Rappites," she said.

I shook my head. "Not really. Religious communities like this always combined the best of devotion and a pioneer spirit. They had to."

We stepped inside one of the smaller living units, just one room, walls hard and thick like bunkers, two windows in one wall, one window in a second wall, rafters and ceiling beams all exposed, more like the shell of a building than the building itself. I wondered if the walls had originally been plastered but there was no one to ask. The weathered oak planks made the room look dark and dungeon-like and I tried to scratch at the oak with my fingernail, but I knew it would be impossible—oak becomes as hard as steel after a century and more. You can't even drive a sixteen-penny nail into such an old piece of oak. But the walls were straight and flat, the floor level, and the ceiling tight. The chinking wasn't original, all concrete now, which felt like cheating, but it was effective, a necessary improvement. A flood would sweep around these buildings but not into them, they were that tight and robust. I just like old buildings, I guess. I respect them.

On my way out of the antique store I nod to the owner but not before I pick up a slim pack of baseball trading cards from the 1980s still in the original waxy paper wrapper, then I drop them back in the box.

Outside I find my bicycle again and pedal easily back toward a bridge that runs over the White River, which is to the west of the courthouse. The river is not deep but fishermen in flat-bottomed boats like to travel up and down the waterway in pursuit of bass, both smallmouth and largemouth, as well as catfish and crappie. I leave the bridge and roll my bicycle carefully down the incline toward the edge of the river, one hand over my bicycle's top tube and the other on the end of the handlebar to guide it. Though it is autumn the dry prairie grass is tall and wild, the current is slow, and an old man in a rocking chair on a deck waves at me from across the way. The day feels special and I wonder why. That's just it—nothing is out of the ordinary, there is nothing to complain about and nothing to do about anything either. Maybe I should sit in a rocking chair on a deck and watch the river slowly flow by myself. My little safari lasts past the next two bridges, then I push my bike up the incline to the main road again, throw my leg over the top tube and start my ride back to a house not quite so empty for there are memories everywhere like those myriad little scraps of paper Jews like to stuff between blocks in their Wailing Wall.

CHAPTER 8

I was surprised that day in 2005 to see the quarter-page display ad in the *Indianapolis Star* for a "teach-in" on the Iraq War. The phrase at first fell flat, a lead clapper in a cracked cast iron bell that clunked rather than rang. Nevertheless I remembered teach-ins. We'd had them at Indiana State during my short tenure there, all about Vietnam then. Students at the elite schools—Harvard, Stanford, Duke—had learned how to beat the draft by 1968 and 1969 so it was the sons of working-class stiffs at regional public universities like Georgia Southern and Eastern Kentucky and Indiana State who were corralled and led into battle, not to mention the kids who'd historically gone straight from high school drop-out to the assembly lines at Motorola and General Electric and Kraft Foods. As I read the full ad I saw that professors still railed against American imperialism, decried our support for Middle East despots, and belittled the multinationals, the new name for an old bugaboo, namely capitalism. Bertrand had been in for about a year when I drove down to IUPUI for the event. I asked Thetis if she wanted to come but she said she had some knitting to complete. Knitting was not merely a pastime; it was her refuge, I think.

IUPUI is an initialism for Indiana University-Purdue University at Indianapolis, the joint commuter campus for the state's two leading public institutions of higher learning. The campus had modest roots years earlier in a leased building near the fairgrounds, literally across from the stables and haylofts and midget-car racing oval, but the college grew and migrated downtown when it was ready for prime time.

I had forgotten how college students dressed before arriving at the night's venue. When I was younger we already had the stringy long hair, the facial stubble, and the denim jeans with torn knees and frayed edges for the boys, yet the button-down shirts and penny loafers, holdovers from the 1950s, still were extant and not retro, and some of the girls still wore blouses with Peter Pan collars and pleated skirts, even shellacked their hair with something they sprayed from a can. Now the preppy look was restricted to a very few Catholic Newman Center students and, of course, a pocketful of Young Republicans. Yoga pants for the girls was not yet a style though.

The crowd inside the lecture hall featured coliseum-like seating with semicircular rows at a steep angle leading down to the stage. Besides the student population I noted the lean older women with dry hair and long scarves around their necks, Modigliani art in decay, as well as men with high foreheads and fierce-looking butch haircuts like Left-leaning Mussolinis. This was not an Indianapolis Colts crowd; it was not *A Sunday Afternoon on the Island of La Grande Jatte* either.

A large pulldown screen atop the stage silently showed grainy black-and-white video clips of exploding smart bombs somewhere in an ancient desert preserve, but presumably Iraq or Afghanistan, along with pictures of fleeing children and grieving mothers in hijabs. This was the human toll for sure but the images reminded me of scattering ants in an arcade video game; so, too, the aged Russian jet fighters plummeting to earth like dead flies, the camera lingering on the billowing smoke in the aftermath of a crash. Nonetheless the mood and chatter of actual, living people inside the lecture hall seemed convivial, even jovial as they stood in aisles or jostled for seats or cried, "Over here," apparently to friends they had hoped to meet at the event like attending some concert.

Several speakers sat in a line on the stage but it was a soldier in uniform among them that seemed out of place to me. The antiwar teach-in had been promoted as nonpartisan but that would be like a religious order saying it's nonsectarian. What I failed to understand at first was that religious orders always like converts and this was no different—presumably the soldier had gone over to the other side, so to speak. Still I was committed to listening and learning. I supported my son and I supported my country, but that did not mean I supported the war. I was hoping to hear other people like me speak up; I hoped they knew more about what was really going on overseas than I did; and I especially hoped everyone would avoid binary thinking and false dichotomies, pretending that one side or another in a debate is ever all right or all wrong.

I saw an open seat in the middle of one row and squeezed between people who already had found their places. I drew a couple of stares as I weaved my way down the aisle and into my seat, possibly because I had short hair neatly parted on the side but a bit fluffy on top, all in all not so different than the late John F. Kennedy look, or perhaps because I'd worn my old Harris tweed sport jacket with suede patches at the elbows, which I had done as a kind of spoof, that being the stereotype of academics when I was younger. It wasn't all that clever, I suppose.

And so it began.

The initial speaker introduced himself—I forget his name now but he taught political science or international relations—and he welcomed us all, said we were patriots as much as Paul Revere was in 1775, except that today the cry should be, "The Fascists are coming! The Fascists are coming." The crowd erupted in assent and delight and I knew I was in for a rip-roaring evening.

"Forty years ago, the first anti-Vietnam War teach-in was held at the University of Michigan," he said. "Today we have teach-ins from Columbia to Stanford, from Ann Arbor to Austin. Again the goal is the same. We all want to stop wars. Some of the arguments both for and against this new war will sound familiar but some are different. 'We're the leader of the Free World'? That delusion hasn't changed. It's just another name for hegemony. 'Saddam Hussein must be stopped'? Well, he is no Ho Chi Minh, but Iraq once was in the grips of imperialists and colonial settlers no less than was Indochina. 'This is a just war'? I think some Americans are genuinely confused on this point. In World War II everyone knew who the good guys were and who the bad guys were. In Vietnam some of us knew—I'm not being an elitist in saying that, it's just that some of us did know. Now it's difficult for some people to accept that we're all bad guys, us and Saddam. That's not a good enough reason for us to be there."

I felt the man was trying to be evenhanded about Iraq though there were no victims of Saddam's regime present to say just *how bad* he was. Speakers followed and they all condemned Bush and Paul Wolfowitz and Condoleezza Rice, chastised Congress, and excoriated our generals.

"How can we give up the lives of all these young men in the name of a lie," said one speaker. "We have to continue speaking truth to power."

"If it was wrong to go into Iraq in 2003, it's wrong to stay there," said another.

A Catholic priest dressed in his full soutane berated our government for making war on Muslims. "Jesus is respected by Islam," he said. "We are all children of Abraham." The man's grief runneth over; he was drowning in his own dolor, his head bent low and arm hooked and fist clenched. But the Jesus to whom he referred would be a Muslim prophet, not the Son of God, I wanted to correct him. And all the children of Abraham would be Muslims, too, or on the right path toward that end. I just wished he'd gotten his theology down a little better and I almost raised my hand as if he might call on me. But what would be the use? As Ingmar Bergman's knight in *The Seventh Seal* said to his valet, "I envy you. You believe your bullshit."

The presence of the American soldier in uniform troubled me most. When he finally was called to the lectern he told of holding comrades in his arms as they lay dying, of looking inside bombed-out buildings while on patrol and not being able to count all the corpses he saw, of crying silently at night so that others in his unit wouldn't hear. He was a witness to hell, he claimed. Maybe so, I thought.

"I saw the exploded belly of a dead pregnant woman," he recalled. "A cold, blue fetus lay just outside the torso, still connected by a limp umbilical cord." Maybe so, maybe so.

The audience was most moved by these depictions. It was a lot like being in a black church—the "call and respond" was overt, people punctuating how awful the imagery was with their own words, cursing Bush and Blair, sprouting their own animal cries and groans, calling for an end to the war "now," but I knew they'd still be going out for drinks later in the evening, still go home to warm beds before the daily grind the next morning. They'd done their duty, hadn't they? They were the antiwar protesters, were they not? Not much different than American flags clipped to the car windows of Fox News patriots, I think.

Again I wanted to speak up. My son was a soldier but he was not there.

Where is your son, Mr. Bogdanovic?
He's in Afghanistan.
What is he doing there?
He's defending your freedom.
Oh, come now.
Well, at least he stepped up.
He just fell for a lie.
And what lie is that?
America.

You see, I was willing to listen to these people, but I didn't think they would be willing to listen to me.

After the event I inadvertently bumped into a young man on my way out. Forget my earlier stereotype of young college students then—he was clean-shaven and dressed in a very ordinary way, technical jacket by North Face and a blue Chicago Cubs cap on his head, not alternative at all. I apologized profusely and he told me to think nothing of it, then I surprised myself by grabbing him by the arm. "I want to ask you a question," I said. The young man looked at me, puzzled for sure, but the tilt of his head told me I could proceed.

"What do you think about the war?" I asked.

His face brightened, he deliberated for a moment, and then he answered me. "Well, I always root for the US in international sports so I hope we win in Iraq."

I could hardly believe my ears.

THIS WAS Bertrand's last visit home, as in the last time I saw him alive. It was on a Saturday afternoon in June of 2012 and he came unannounced; I was in the driveway washing the car when I saw him. An occasional bicyclist passed on the street in our quiet neighborhood and a mother pushing a pram had come down the sidewalk a little earlier. It was that kind of pleasant, forgettable day. I had my hand in a pail of soapy water as I clutched a big yellow sponge and out of the corner of my eye I saw him casually coming up the street on foot, a duffel bag tossed over his shoulder. It was like seeing a ship coming into port after a long sea voyage, one moment it's not on the horizon and the next moment it is, and I could feel Bertrand coming closer. I was in his presence already.

"How you doin', Pops," Bertrand said as he dropped his bag on the grass. I stood erect and wet my lips, then I stretched out my arms. The sun was very bright that day.

I suggested we go inside, "Let's tell Mother that you're home." We did and Thetis hurriedly prepared a fruit salad from apple slices, cantaloupe, and black cherries.

"I can bring out the fine china," she said. We always wanted to remain calm when Bertrand was home, not show that we were ever worried, but inevitably our exuberance bubbled over. Bertrand lifted a plate that Thetis already had put out and noted that it was Corelle.

"I remember when you bought this set," he said as he returned the plate to the table. Thetis had laid a green tattersall cloth before setting out the plates and cutlery. "Target, right? Never buy more than you need."

"I can bake a pie," Thetis said. "I have pecans and a frozen pie crust."

"Sit down, Mother," Bertrand told her. Confidently, lovingly, appreciatively.

We'd kept a bedroom for our son the entire time he was gone, but that's not unusual. Thetis or I would dust in there weekly and change the bedspread and sheets with the seasons, and after our light snack Bertrand said he needed to nap. He told us he could stay only a very brief time and I counted the hours, even the minutes, in my head; I savored every moment even though I knew that doesn't make time last longer, that all you ever end up with is memories. I wanted to fill the brief time we would have with him, to do things, but what? From the mundane like going to the movies to flying a kite like we used to do when he was a child, I conjured frivolous possibilities as I sat in a chair near his bed. I had gone upstairs after he was asleep because I wanted to be sure his breathing was even and steady, which was what Thetis or I would do when he was a baby. I'd pulled the blinds shut and as I sat at Bertrand's side I noticed how broad his shoulders were, how perfectly placed his head was on a pillow much like a crown on a red velvet cushion.

Maybe we'll have dinner out, all three of us, I thought. I knew I was being silly but it was only normal—if you have a guest in the house you want to do things, to show the person a good time.

A guest? I had to stop myself. But he was a guest, a mysterious visitor, little more than an apparition. Later that evening Bertrand said he had to go out to meet someone and that was fine with us. It was all borrowed time.

"Old girlfriend?" I teased.

"Don't wait up," he replied, and he asked for the keys to the car.

I speculated on just what he was up to, or into, and of course we waited up, Thetis until about one A.M. after which I insisted she go to bed, and I until about three A.M. I couldn't imagine he was on official business, not here in Indianapolis, but I hardly knew his business anymore. It's funny how you look at yourself in a mirror and you don't look that old, but then you see yourself in a photograph and you wonder who is that old man. It's the same thing with your children—you look at them and it's an amalgam of all their faces over the years but melded into one that, among other things, makes them look younger than they are, younger than they would appear to anyone else.

It had to be an old girlfriend, I concluded. A boy like Bertrand must have had many even if I'd only known a couple of them. I was glad he could make it home and I wasn't jealous that he took time out to look someone up. It's the normal thing to do; I even thought I'd ask him who it was when he got back home. Being curious is normal too. I was wakened when Bertrand came in about four A.M. I was going to wake Thetis, too, tell her all is well, but you don't disturb someone's sleep just to say all is well, do you?

On Sunday morning Thetis asked if Bertrand wanted to attend church services with her. When he looked up doubtfully she told him they had a late-morning service with guitars if he'd prefer that, and he asked if we'd become Unitarian Universalists. "Well, you can pray in your own way anywhere, I suppose," she said. "That's what John the Baptist did. But I like the fellowship of organized religion."

Bertrand and I stayed in that morning and I brewed a pot of coffee, then we went out on the back porch. The sun still was low, all the trees on the tree line including the

still extant cottonwood beefy and leafy, and we sat in real
Adirondack chairs I'd ordered from a store in Vermont.
Bertrand wore only thin pajama bottoms tied at the waist
with a drawstring, his long, sinewy torso and arms on full
display.

"When'd you last get a haircut?" I asked. The question
now strikes me as a completely incongruous thing to have
brought up, but his hair looked shaggy in the back of his
head, at least for a soldier. I hadn't noticed it the day before.
"We can go down to Great Clips. They're open on Sundays."

"You still have the clippers you bought when I was
younger?" he asked. I took that to mean he didn't want a
haircut because I'd never given him one that he liked and
I'd stopped insisting on cutting his hair by the time he was
ten or eleven. I then offered him a cigarette and he asked if
Thetis really let me smoke in or around the house. I told him
I didn't light up often, that I kept a box of Winstons inside a
plastic sandwich bag just so they'd stay fresh, and that Thetis
and I had an understanding anyway. He said he never took
up the habit.

"Not in the service? Not even once?" I asked.

"We don't smoke," he repeated, and I took especial note
of the first person plural pronoun. He was proud of his unit
and there'd been a trace of irritation in his retort, or maybe
it had been a rebuke.

I changed the subject and asked Bertrand how much
longer he expected to be in the army. We hadn't discussed his
future in the service much after he'd enlisted and suddenly
that seemed an omission in my thinking, a real dereliction of
my parental role. "I mean, it's important work you're doing,
isn't it?" He was just silent, looking around at the boughs in
the trees and any little floating thing in the warm air around
us. "Is it a calling? Is that why you stay in?"

I realized I was starting to sound needy so I stopped. I offered to get Bertrand some orange juice or a beer and he just shook his head. "Is there anything you want to talk about?" I asked. Finally he stretched out his hand to touch me and even though he could not reach across the outdoor table I understood the gesture well enough. Then he asked me a question that surprised: Had I ever read Ivan Turgenev's *Fathers and Sons*? I told him I had, a long time ago at Indiana State, but not in the original Russian, which I meant as a kind of joke. He told me he'd read it straight through one night in Afghanistan after a load of books came in via a library in Pennsylvania. His copy was a hardback and still had the old-fashioned library card and pocket with dates going back many years. Bertrand wanted to know what I thought of the book. I demurred that I could hardly be expected to remember much of it but I said that I thought a book like that wouldn't find a publisher today because it was so melodramatic and slow-moving, what with its spurned lovers and strained relationships and tragic, unforeseen deaths. It would read like a soap opera script.

"And the theme of the novel? What did you think of that?" Bertrand asked.

"You mean the fathers and sons angle?"

He shook his head. "No hidden agenda here, Dad. I know you love me and I know you know I love you. No issues saying it either. But I don't mean Arkady Kirsanov and his father, Nikolai. I mean Bazarov and his nihilism."

I sighed, a kind of, "Ah, yes," meme. Well, nihilism, what is it really? That's what I said to Bertrand too. "Nihilism, what is it really? That nothing matters, or that we don't know what matters?"

Bertrand nodded. "That's what I've read about nihilism, too, but that's not what I saw in the book. Bazarov was a scientist so evidence and data mattered to him, but only that. Yet Francis Bacon had already embraced empiricism and he wasn't a nihilist."

"So what was nihilism to Bazarov?"

"He saw that bullshit didn't matter, including the church, but also philosophy and the study of ethics and even meaning, trying to figure out the meaning of anything. Science only mattered to him because you could at least document things, actually prove things, and maybe even change outcomes in the real world if you were of a mind to. He liked science because it gets results. But war gets results, too, you know. It's everything else that is just talk. That's what nihilism really is."

I didn't know if I agreed with that but I wasn't about to argue anything with Bertrand. I just knew the book was, in fact, about fathers and sons.

Bertrand showered and dressed, after which I heard him make a couple of phone calls but couldn't make out to whom or what they were about, and when he came down he asked if he could borrow the car again. Of course, I told him, then I asked him where he was going. "Work," he said.

"Work?"

He smiled ironically. I didn't understand his expression at all. It was inscrutable, even cold. "I have to kill someone," he said. "You know, an execution."

"You have to kill someone? Here? In Indianapolis?"

"Unfinished business."

We were in the front hall and he was about to put on his shoes and I almost asked him what time he'd be home *after work* but he was talking about killing someone. I wondered if he'd brought home a gun with him, then I questioned whether he needed to work with a gun. I was very confused by it all.

"I don't think there are any Taliban in Indianapolis, Bertrand," I finally said.

He looked me straight in the eye but his eyelids were heavy, or maybe weary is the word. "Tell Mom I love her," he said. I knew he meant business; I knew he had a mission to complete. I got the car keys and placed them in his hand, which I grasped tightly in mine. As he walked out the front door I followed him with my eyes and then I ran after him as he slid into the front seat of the car.

"What if you get caught?" I asked. "What should I tell the police?" He smiled, a kind of *Oh, you silly fool, if you only knew* look, but not contemptuous or hurtful at all.

"I don't get caught," he said.

"But what if there are cameras? There's cameras everywhere these days. You can't be sure. What if you leave DNA? You sneeze and there'll be DNA."

"If I get caught I'll be released inside of thirty minutes."

"They'll just let you go? Just like that? 'Oh, sorry, Mr. Bogdanovic. Our bad.'"

"They'll make a phone call and then they'll let me go."

"They'll make a call? Call whom?"

Yes, of course, they'd make a call and they'd let him go. "I assume you're supposed to kill this person, whoever it is," I said.

"Well, it's really fucked up," Bertrand said.

"What's fucked up?" I asked.

"This business. It's really fucked up."

"What's fucked up about it?"

"It's fucked up. That's what's fucked up."

I received a call several hours later. Bertrand said he'd left the car near a Ramada Inn and told me he'd be taking a bus out of town, then flying off from another city. He wouldn't tell me more. "It's better that you don't know, just like in the spy novels," he said. *"As-salamu alaykum."*

Of course, of course, I said to myself after he hung up, and I noticed only then that he was calling from some crappy disposable cell phone with a curious area code. I had to figure out what I would say to Thetis but I just told her that our son was called away suddenly and he sent his love and she didn't ask me anything further.

The next day I heard on the news that a body had been found among the detritus that clogs a bend in the White River just south of the Indianapolis Zoo. The police could not immediately identify the deceased individual and were seeking witnesses to the crime but there wouldn't be any.

Of course, of course.

CHAPTER 9

Thetis had given birth to Bertrand a little late in life. The announcement of his coming was simple enough—no coy posturing and suppressed smiles, no frenetic talk of cribs and cabinet locks and boiling baby bottles, no riot of activity at all. We didn't speak of getting a bigger house and we didn't rush to get his name on waiting lists for the best Montessori schools—well, we joked about the latter, plotting how we might go to a nursery school dressed in dirty scrubs and a Stormy Kromer plaid cap, respectively, but only to see the discombobulation on everyone's face. Though Bertrand did not come along so soon after we married we'd been paragons of patience if nothing else. We always believed it would happen eventually. Perhaps Thetis trusted in the Lord a bit but I just figured the odds were with us. I was thirty-six, Thetis thirty-seven.

When Thetis's baby bump was apparent the other nurses fussed over her, of course, and there was no shortage of wise counsel including family traditions that had been passed down over generations. "Breastfeeding burns five hundred calories a day," one pediatric nurse told her. Thetis loved it.

"Always put a teaspoon of white vinegar in baby's bath," an orderly told her. "It stops the hives." I don't think we tested that hypothesis.

Thetis would come home on some days with little gifts—booties, union suits, boxes of disposable diapers (which she donated; she was intent on using cloth "nappies"), and lots of Little Golden Books. "You'll read to our son as much as I will," Thetis said. "Then he'll read to us and we'll listen very attentively." It was the usual assortment of classics—*Goodnight Moon, The Poky Little Puppy*, and *Mickey and the Beanstalk*, plus books for when he was a little older, *Lassie Come-Home* and *The Wind in the Willows*.

I never got to know many of Thetis's colleagues very well even though she'd been at the same hospital for years. They hosted annual Christmas parties for families of employees but the events were far too big and impersonal for me to enjoy. There was no way to meet everyone, to wade through the weeds, as it were, and inevitably the bigwigs would be formally introduced, then they'd make speeches about how much they appreciated such a fine and dedicated staff and what exciting plans were in store for the coming year.

My parents approved of Thetis very much; more than that, they liked her very much. I remember the first time I introduced her to them. She shook their hands and looked past my mother's shoulders and immediately said what a lovely home she had. "Is that a Willett sideboard?" she asked, referring to a furniture piece in the dining room. Thetis wasn't showing off her knowledge; she just knew that Willett was a favorite regional brand from Louisville. I thought it was more important that Thetis get to know my mother than my father and it wasn't because of any stale mother-in-law jokes one still heard from Las Vegas comedians. I think it was because each sex shares something the other sex can never understand. For women it's childbirth; for men it's war.

We had a nice dinner that night. My mother cooked and served and Dad poured the wine. Thetis asked about work on the trains and had I been a good boy growing up.

"I don't know," my father said. "Better ask him."

We all were in a fine mood and when my mother said she'd be serving tea Thetis insisted on helping. It wasn't that everyone was acting proper; we were proper.

I'd met her parents, of course, which was a bit of a fraught experience. The Stantons were more middle class than my folks—he was in management with US Rubber, which still had a large presence in Indianapolis at the time, and Mrs. Stanton belonged to a women's club and played golf, yet here I was, a college dropout and sporting goods salesman, retail at that. Mr. Stanton liked to hunt and fish up around Idaho and Montana and he knew a lot about equipment but he didn't try to make me feel small, at least not too much. Thetis had warned me that he was a deacon in his church and I might be quizzed a little. "He's big on guidance," she told me. "Every man needs a guide." I'd argue with people about religion when I felt like it and there were times I might have to push back against outright proselytizing, but this was my future father-in-law we were talking about.

After marrying, Thetis and I would often take moonlight walks in the months leading up to the birth of our son, holding hands and looking at the stars, that classic gesture, and thinking about what our boy might be like as an adult. We'd known it would be a boy since the eighteenth or nineteenth week. I decided then I would help him in any way I could yet stop short of trying to mold him in my own image like some vengeful, selfish god. It wouldn't be right to seek immortality through one's son even if it could be done.

Thetis stayed home until Bertrand started school—she was the cook and the homemaker and the keel while I took care of the car and the yard and the bills and never failed to show up for my job on time. It was she who volunteered much more than I did and who roped me in occasionally. I did hammering and drilling for Habitat for Humanity, helped stock a local food bank, and even was a bell ringer for the Salvation Army one year. We were peers because of how blue our loyalty to each other was, how plumb we always were with each other. Then I had a different insight. It was as if we'd always been married, as in I couldn't remember a time that we weren't married. We were transcendental and it was this feeling of forever that was to become a test of true love for me.

Though I've always been a bit of a loner—individual sports such as bicycling, swimming, or hiking didn't just begin after I lost her—Thetis was more focused on groups, things like book clubs and church families and even quilting bees. I found her lifestyle complementing mine quite squarely as I rarely was expected to join in her activities and I wasn't cornered into feeling guilt when I went out on my own. She often invited guests over to the house, of course, and I was almost like the help in those situations, bringing out a silver tray with tea and petit fours or just introducing myself formally before excusing myself, "Well, I'll just leave you girls alone then" or words like that. If Bertrand was home he'd also say hello and answer their questions about school or sports, and sometimes he and I would retire to our respective rooms and sometimes we'd have an excuse to go out on our own. Yet Thetis became more engrossed in her extracurricular activities after Bertrand left for the army, which was a telling thing for me to see. One might have thought we'd be spending more time together but that was not the case. Maybe she wasn't so trusting in the Lord after all. Or was she secretly angry at me for letting our son join the army in a time of war, him living up to his grandfather's and great-grandfather's legacy, not mine? We always looked forward to mail from our son, eagerly unfolding the handwritten notes on crisp paper like children at Christmas, sometimes taking turns reading them aloud, but they had become more somber in tone over time, darker and more biting; they were like wounds seeping resentment and disillusionment.

Bertrand had begun making critical analyses of his role in the military, of the military's role in society, even the meaning of the nation's support for soldiers like him. By critical I just mean he sought to understand. One late letter was the most contemptuous yet:

> "The Secretary of Defense visited Bagram today. Lots of media were there and they grouped some of the soldiers in a kind of circular patch around him for the photo op. He told us how brave we all were and how much America appreciates our service. They kept the Afghan National Army guys way back; everyone is afraid of Taliban infiltrators, of course. And I just read where Prince Harry was withdrawn from Afghanistan. Yes, he'd be a juicy hostage for the Taliban. At least he came here. But do I really have to listen to the Secretary of Defense tell us how much America appreciates our service? Well, I'd like to appreciate his service, the NFL's service, Coca-Cola's service, my high school valedictorian's service, and the gym teacher's service too. I'd even like to appreciate the Afghan National Army's service. But some of the Afghanis do fight, some of them, at least. And my buddies fight. I believe in my buddies and I believe they believe in me but I'm losing faith in the mission. Those who stay and fight only do so to prove something to themselves. Either that, or they're fools."

I often studied Thetis as she sat in the evenings in her easy chair reading a chapter in a book or just working on her needlepoint, the genial light from a small table lamp at her side casting her face in bas-relief profile. Thetis had been raised in a religious, even doctrinaire home. Belief in God was a given and she was taught by her father to look down on atheists though her mother urged her to "give a hand up" to people who hadn't found their way yet. Thetis often said she loved God for the comfort her belief gave her. When I said that wasn't proof of his existence she said that if nothing else God was in the beholding, which was enough truth for her. When I asked if she trusted in the Lord to protect our Bertrand when he went into battle she said it was out of her hands, that that was a kind of belief in God too.

Thetis often would bring home stories from work, though she'd always announce that she was changing the names of the patients involved to protect their confidentiality, which I thought was sweet but quite unnecessary within the family. It was just Thetis being Thetis. Most of the stories dealt with passages—a new birth if she was working in the nursery, witnessing last rites for an elderly patient, or a hysterectomy or mastectomy for any young woman. "Grace" was a big issue with her, as in people who confronted their fate with grace, which she also thought was a sign of their own godliness. "Mr. Pilkington died today," she told me once. "His family had come to visit earlier in the day. They brought him chocolates and a *Sports Illustrated* and photos of his grandson, who made Eagle Scout. When he wanted a drink of water they poured him water from a glass pitcher and when he wanted more light in the room they pulled open the curtains. 'It's all I want,' he told them, and then he said he wanted to nap. After they left he fell asleep and he died a little while later."

I remember taking Thetis to visit the old L. S. Ayres store in Indianapolis, albeit renamed and under new management by then. The original store closed in 1992, after my mother had died. It sat empty for three years while a two-city-block area that included the building was being renovated to put up a hybrid downtown mall that included some original structures and street elevations along with new construction. In time a regional department store chain named Parisian claimed the Ayres property and opened its own store in the same space in 1995. The change wasn't worth much, just more merchandise on more racks and almost everything made offshore by then. Nevertheless we decided to visit the new store and mall soon after its grand opening one Saturday afternoon. I thought I'd buy Thetis a new dress or some other pretty thing, something just for her, nothing she really needed or would ever buy on her own, I knew. She was the kind of person who always thought gifts came as good deeds, not frivolous things, that they had to come from the heart and not from the pocketbook. While I didn't disagree with that I did have to ask sometimes what's wrong with a pretty thing?

Every city of considerable size once had a grand department store with life-size displays in the front plate-glass windows that changed with the seasons, knowledgeable buyers who'd visit all the trade shows and vouch for all the merchandise on the sales floors, and especially a tea room. Maybe not in the English style, service at certain times only, but you'd be seated at handcrafted tables and enjoy a light repast on fine china plates and crystal glassware, and you might even be entertained live by a competent musician at a quality piano. The Ayres tea room had all of that, but not in Parisian. The new store just had vending machines down a hall. No matter. The merchandise was all right at first but then the

quality began to slowly sink to near Walmart levels as a new
generation of Americans didn't know what good quality was
anymore, so why try to get them to pay for it.

I always thought Thetis looked best in light blue or lav-
ender, perhaps with an emerald or jade accessory that would
highlight her dress, along with smooth leather shoes featuring
a low vamp and perhaps an almond toe, nothing too pointy.
Mom would speak about women's fashions when she worked
at the store but I'd forgotten most of it over the years. Still I
wanted Thetis to dress up sometimes and I told her we were
going to buy her a new dress the day we visited Parisian.

Thetis had a long, oval-shaped face and she wore her
hair in an old-fashioned schoolmarmish style in those days,
cut long but tightly pulled back and tied in a neat bun. I
admit to liking it that way—the look was serious but not
stern, intelligent but not superior, prudent but not reluctant.
There's always strength in not showing too much. And yet
there was so much femininity in reserve when she wore her
hair like that, or dressed in a wool pencil skirt and an ivory
silk blouse, and I loved it when we'd come home from a night
out, however infrequent that might have been, and she'd
untie her bun and flip her head back while she ran through
her hair with her fingers, then spin quickly on the balls of
her feet to face me before revealing herself further. It could
only mean one thing.

Thetis chose three dresses to try on and I watched as she
held them close to her chest while standing in front of the
three-way mirror. She turned her head slightly left and right
to view the different angles and she switched back and forth
among the different choices. "Which do you like?" she asked
without turning to look at me, though perhaps she caught
sight of me at the edge of one of the mirrors. I told her I
liked them all and she rejected that answer. "Dwight, I won't

try on any of them unless you tell me which you like best."
She wasn't being demanding; she just didn't like it when
someone was evasive. One dress featured a polka dot bodice
over a dark navy skirt that was slightly flared—I remember
eliminating that one first. A long, satiny dress with ruffles at
the hem seemed too Southern, too beauty pageant-like for
me and so I rejected that next. It was not quite a process of
elimination though. I liked the third, a lemon-yellow color
with a subtle crosshatch pattern with white threads, very
summery and jaunty.

Thetis liked the dress, too, and it fit well so we bought it.
I suggested having it sent to our address and she asked why
would we do that for such a small package and I said the
well-heeled ladies of old always demanded home delivery.
My mother had told me that—the customers would closely
inspect her as she'd wrap a small garment in tissue, then
place it into a smart-looking box, and tie a string around it.
The box would always be addressed to a "Miss" or "Mrs.,"
sometimes to a "Dr. and Mrs.," then the package would be
delivered the same day in a panel truck Ayres itself owned if
parcel post wasn't fast enough. Ayres didn't do that for small
packages anymore by the time I worked there but Mom still
talked about it. Alas, the sales clerk at Parisian didn't know
what I was talking about when I brought it up and Thetis
said she would have eschewed that option in any case.

Afterward we stopped for drinks at a new bar in the new
mall—there were a lot of people about so maybe downtown
shopping had become a novelty by 1995—and then we dined
at the Eagle's Nest, a revolving restaurant atop the tallest
hotel in the city. The waiter welcomed us with a wink—
maybe we looked like people who didn't get out much—and
he seated us in the outer rim of the circular room, that is, at
a window facing the world. It was just before twilight when

we arrived, which is the best time from on high to catch the violet and blue light scatter in the sky, the burning lamp bulbs below and the still discernible facades of all the visible buildings. Everything just looks dreamier then; it's why photographers always do their night shots a few minutes before the sun sets so they can pick up as much detail as possible and still imply the dark.

We each ordered wine to start and made small talk—*Were we happy? Had we wanted more children? Will we remember this night for a long time?*—and I thought of Maurice Chevalier and Hermione Gingold in *Gigi*. Maybe we would recall this incidental evening one day and Thetis would have to correct my recollections so that I would have to say, "Yes, I remember it well."

Well, I remember it, how relaxed yet steady her demeanor was as she leaned on her elbows looking down on the city, how velvety her skin was in the subtle light, and how lucky I was to have met her, how she had made me so even with life. She was more than I thought.

THE MAIL comes early in my neighborhood and I can always tell the exact time it arrives by the growl from those boxy delivery trucks the post office uses as the driver accelerates from one mailbox to the next. It's the usual collection of nonprofit pitches and advertising fliers but also a small padded envelope. I toss everything save the small padded envelope into a wastebasket, then I neatly tear open the latter to reveal a handwritten note that has been folded over in half as well as something small wrapped inside tissue. "Dear Mr. Bogdanovic," the letter begins. "You don't know me but I knew your son, Bertrand. I was with him that weekend in Indianapolis when he made the kill."

I'd never spoken to anyone about the murder, even Thetis, but not counting the two detectives who had come to our door to question me about it several weeks after the event. The dead man, who'd eventually been identified in the press as Corporal Carl Hennessey, was a member of Bertrand's company when he was still in the regular army. With a large enough database, it was easy to connect the dots, for the police to pay a call. "Did you know the deceased?" they asked. I told them I knew nothing. "Was your son home around the time of the murder?" Again I told them I knew nothing. The policemen, two burly, somewhat sloppily dressed guys with thinning crew cut hairstyles, probably veterans themselves, were suspicious, I'm sure. But they didn't come back. I never told Bertrand about their visit. I was all about leaving no paper trail, no phone records, no electronic footprints. But maybe I secretly hoped it wasn't Bertrand who had done this thing after all.

It was a four-page letter written in a tight script on lined paper; the letter writer, who identified herself as Theresa Taylor, said she'd met my son during basic training in Columbus, Georgia, and they'd remained friends. She noted that they'd once seen a French movie in an art house cinema in Atlanta together and that they'd honored a picket line thrown up by striking housekeepers at a hotel in Montgomery, Alabama. I think she was trying to establish her bona fides by relating these things, to show me that she and Bertrand had a special relationship. She claimed that Bertrand would write her from overseas after he was deployed, muses about minarets silhouetted against a setting sun or descriptions of whisper trails in the night sky, but sometimes he'd just ask her to please remind him of what normal people still do in America such as go to the theater or play touch football with friends on a Thanksgiving morning.

"Now this is what I have to tell you," Theresa Taylor wrote. "Bertrand told me about an incident in Afghanistan. He said there was a Carl Hennessey also from Indianapolis who was a new member of his unit when he was in Helmand Province and he proved to be very disruptive, always complaining and whining about something. Bertrand called him a real blowhard, someone who talked tough but hadn't seen any combat yet like the other boys had. Bertrand said he was the kind of guy who could get everyone killed if he acted too rashly. And after the first firefight he was in, Hennessey apparently shit his pants. He cowered while the other boys had to push back a coordinated attack from three sides on their FOB. That's a Forward Operating Base and they called it Blue Ridge because that's how everything looked at night. I can imagine what they all said to Hennessey after the battle was over. *What the fuck's the matter with you, Hennessey? Where were you, Hennessey? We don't ever want to see you again, Hennessey.* Actually, that's exactly what everyone told him, Bertrand wrote. Well, Hennessey ran away a few weeks later and the unit had to go out searching for him. Bertrand and the others knew how to track someone and they found out where he was but Hennessey had been captured by some locals and they were holding him until the Taliban could come get him. When Bertrand and the others went to rescue him, there was an ambush and two men in Bertrand's company were killed and several others wounded. This was in some backward village with mud houses and dirt streets, but they had electricity and when the unit was spotted, someone lit a spotlight and people just started shooting at them. Bertrand said they had to blow up some houses and if Hennessey was in one of them so be it but he wasn't. They later learned that more than twenty villagers had been killed in what the Afghan government called an unprovoked raid and President Karzai

protested to the US government. You probably heard about
that part of the story. It was all over in the media and our
government profusely apologized and offered to pay com-
pensation to the victims' families. But the important detail
missing from all the reporting was that the team was looking
for a deserter and they'd got him too. Mission accomplished,
right? But we covered up that part of the operation. Hennessey had never run away, like it never happened. The government was even going to court-martial Bertrand and the
other boys for the Afghan deaths but they stopped short of
that. They should have court-martialed Hennessey. Instead
they gave him a general discharge. It's not a dishonorable
discharge. It just means you're not in the army anymore.
And they disbanded the unit, closed the FOB for good. That
was to satisfy Karzai so he'd have something to crow about.
Bertrand told me he was going to quit the army over it but
then he was recruited into special ops. Those people knew
he was someone who gets the job done. He was relentless."

I remembered the story about all those civilian deaths
in Helmand Province. No names of American soldiers ever
were released and Bertrand had never written me about
those events. There'd been quite a few reports like that over
the years and I always told myself that the other side committed more atrocities anyway as if that was the only metric
that mattered. Theresa Taylor was about to surprise me further though.

"Do you believe in coincidences, Mr. Bogdanovic?" the
letter continued. "For I knew Carl Hennessey myself. I guess
I always liked soldiers, manly men, you could say. I'd moved
to Indianapolis and I was working as a pharmacy tech for
Walgreens and living in Broad Ripple. Have you ever been
there? I would do the club scene on Friday and Saturday
nights and I met Carl one evening and we hit it off. He was

a big, good-looking guy with a big grin and thick, wavy hair
that he let grow long, at least after he got out of the service.
He told me all about his battles and stuff and I believed him
because he had all the terminology down pat and he knew
things most civilians don't. Well, when Bertrand wrote and
told me what the real story was I had to tell him that I knew
Carl Hennessey. Bertrand wrote back and asked if I knew
how to find Carl. Well, Carl Hennessey and I had had a
relationship. We'd stayed together for quite a while but then
he started becoming very possessive. He wasn't working or
he'd start a job and say it sucked and then he'd quit after two
weeks and stay home and drink a lot and watch TV. I had to
work late sometimes at Walgreens and that's when he started
acting suspicious. Do you ever watch those wife-beating epi-
sodes on *Dr. Phil* or *Jerry Springer*? It was just like that. When
I told him I was going to leave him he nearly whipped me
to death. I finally sicced the police on him. I really did. Got
a restraining order and everything. Funny thing is, he got
a lawyer through some veterans group, pleaded guilty to a
misdemeanor, and agreed to stay away from me. He never
went to jail or anything. Carl would write me from time to
time and ask to get together again and I said I hoped he got
better but I had moved on.

"I asked Bertrand why he wanted to see Carl and he told
me the rest of the story from Blue Ridge. He said that after
the rescue, after it was announced that the unit was being
disbanded, he and some of the other boys made a pact.
They drew lots and the one with the lowest number would
have to kill Carl Hennessey when he could. I didn't believe
that part of the story at first but then I thought maybe it was
true. I understood what Hennessey had put them through.
But I wouldn't tell Bertrand where to find Carl. I didn't want
to be a part of anything crazy like that. I didn't hear from

Bertrand again for months and then he wrote to tell me that he would be visiting Indianapolis soon and he really wanted to see me. I figured we were just going to spend the night together but then he asked me again if I knew where to find Carl. I knew I shouldn't have told him but I couldn't help myself in the end. He was Bertrand, after all. Well, after I told him he got up and said he had to go but that he wanted to give me something first, something he'd been keeping since his childhood. He said he'd worn it sometimes with his dog tag when he used to wear a dog tag and when I saw it I thought it was a walnut shell but it was a baby turtle shell. Bertrand had drilled a small hole in the top so he could put it on a steel ball chain too. He had it wrapped in tissue and he pressed it into my hand and he said I should keep it 'just in case.' I asked if he was serious about killing Carl Hennessey and if that's what he meant, that something would go wrong or he'd get caught and he said he wasn't going to get caught because things like this happen in the military and everybody knows it but that I should send it to his parents in case something happened to him later on. 'I'm trusting you with this, Theresa,' he told me. I hope you can forgive me for not sending it sooner.

"When I heard about Carl's death on the TV I didn't say anything to anyone, but the police did come around to interview me. We had lived together so it couldn't have been that hard to figure it out. The police asked me if Carl had any enemies and I said none that I knew of. They asked if he was involved in any illegal activities, maybe like bringing heroin back from Afghanistan, and I said not that I knew of. I was so afraid they were going to ask me about Bertrand but they never did. Maybe I didn't write you before because I didn't want to draw attention to Bertrand. The government reads mail sometimes, you know.

"One last thing. I do visit Bertrand's grave at Crown Hill Cemetery on occasion. Someone used to lay flowers there but not in the last few years that I've noticed. I should have picked up on that sooner. I think I will start leaving flowers. And I'm married now. Theresa Taylor was my maiden name. I hope you will forgive me but I don't want to give you my married name. And I don't work at Walgreens anymore. I think it's better if we leave it this way. I would like to know what the turtle shell means but I guess I never will."

CHAPTER 10

I only wanted to have enough money to live on all the years I worked at the sporting goods store, enough to keep Thetis and Bertrand fed and warm at night. I don't see that it was a bad life—not everyone reaches the mountaintop and not everyone should try. Chasing mechanical rabbits around a dog track is futile too. I was satisfied helping fit kids with a good baseball glove each spring and I'd play a little toss-and-catch with them to be sure, or I'd take a child out in the employee parking lot and let him or her test ride a bicycle while Mom waited nervously at the curb, knuckles to mouth, or Dad would be there with his video camera to make memories of the occasion. My sporting goods store was bright, airy, well-stocked and even friendly, a garden of delights for the active person. No, it wasn't like the neighborhood sports stores of yore on the town square or at the six-corners in a bigger city that took their orders from the local high school coaches, changed stock seasonally, and never offered discounts or rewards cards, but it was all right. I did wax nostalgic sometimes for those olden days, though, when you knew that a Rawlings glove came from Saint Louis, Converse All Stars were made in Malden, Massachusetts, and Schwinn bikes were still made in Chicago—of course! They say the

Indians sold Manhattan Island to the settlers for twenty-four dollars worth of trinkets; now we're selling America for even less.

The diurnal rhythms of working in a retail store had their charm. Staff would come in before customers, obviously, but it's all a little like getting ready for show time. You'd turn on the lights, check the aisles for loose or misplaced merchandise, and turn your head from time to time at the brightening parking lot and any people in silhouette who might be headed to the large, automatic glass doors. I think I saw a movie once that featured a scene with men and women who worked in an upscale retail store and maybe it was in America or maybe it was a European film. I think they sped up the film a little but everyone was dressed in dark suits with crisp white shirts and they'd dust the countertops and all the displays, position everything in place as if checking the alignment on a wall hanging, and then they'd stand at attention until an actual customer appeared. We weren't quite like that at Dick's, the salesmen and women being more chatty among themselves, asking about each other's children, or how was that date last night if it were the younger sales associates, maybe complaining about the rush of customers that might be expected if there was a good sale on.

Thetis would send some of her fellow nurses or their husbands to seek me out for guidance. I didn't much appreciate that. I didn't work on commission, for one thing, so what was the point, and maybe I was self-conscious about "only" being a salesman. "It's like being fitted for a good suit," Thetis would tell me. "You want a good salesperson, not just someone who says, 'That suits you' or 'That's a very good choice,' then laughs at you behind your back." I gave her the benefit of the doubt.

Bertrand would come down to the store and hang out sometimes when he was younger. A couple of the other sales associates did resent that—they were working while I was having fun with my son—and a manager once brought it up, but I liked it when Bertrand would help me put all the hang cards on the right hooks and sort all the different balls in the right bins and so on. Sometimes he'd just hang out in the break room until my shift was over, do his homework or play with a handheld video game, and in fact some of the other workers would send him two doors down in the shopping center to a sandwich shop to buy them a meal. This was mostly when he was in fifth and sixth grade, a good time to be someone's son and run errands for his friends. Having purpose in life has to start somewhere.

Sometimes we got to test equipment, though usually only returned items that we couldn't resell. I remember the kayak that one customer said wouldn't travel straight but he'd run it in a very shallow stream and the bottom was scratched. A manager had to approve the return. "Let's see if he was right," I suggested when I saw the kayak stored on the rear loading dock. We were going to have it recycled. I tied it to the roof of my car with nylon rope. The kayak wasn't going to do any damage to the car, or vice versa—we always promoted those things as being made from the same material as laundry detergent bottles and it was true.

Bertrand was excited when he saw me come home with the watercraft. "Where we goin', Pops?" he asked. The answer was Sugar Creek, a winding waterway in west-central Indiana that travels through Turkey Run State Park, between deep canyon walls, and beyond. What would just be a fun day out for me would be a great adventure for a kid, of course, like Marquette and Joliet, even Lewis and Clark.

Budding entomologists should come to Indiana and ride its rivers and creeks—diaphanously winged bugs skim the bubbly, broken surface of all the shallow streams in search of prey and hover and dive and stalk smaller bugs all along the leafy banks. I've seen pictures of bigger insects in the Amazon but those were only pictures; these native Hoosier insects were a real and present danger, almost as thick as hail at times. We paddled upstream first, of course, so that we could mostly float back to the car after we reached the far-thest place. It was a two-seater kayak and we both had pad-dles but I sat in back all the way up and down and cheated, only lightly pushing the blades of my paddle in the water as Bertrand earned his stripes.

"So, Dad, what do you think about all day when you're at work?" Bertrand asked me at one point. We'd just spot-ted a deer in the forest beyond and Bertrand let the kayak glide while the deer seemed to study us, then it scurried off at the crack of a tree limb over its head. The boy had been exhibiting increasing inquisitiveness about the world—its vastness, its mysteries, its objects—and I think that included me. Imagine you're sitting in a theater and a stage play is being presented and there are sets and props and lighting and curtains and especially the players. The dialogue, the action too. Now imagine that the other theatergoers in seats all around you also are, in their own way, participants in the play. Only you are outside of the action and only what you think matters. This is not solipsism; the world outside your head does exist. But that's exactly the point. What do you make of this world outside your head? It would take awhile to figure things out, wouldn't it? That's an inquisitive child.

Bertrand's question struck me like a shaft of light, like a blazing reflection of the sun on the surface of the water itself. This was not a "take your child to work day" question.

It was not even whether I liked my job or not. What *did* I think about all day? It was the deepest of philosophical questions. If I think, therefore I am. If so, am I what I think about? And if I don't think about anything then am I nothing again?

But that is all to dodge Bertrand's question, one that bedevils me to this day. What did I think about all day at work? Work to be done—sure. Inventorying, showing people where the running shorts or fishing lures could be found, "Follow me," and all that—sure. Helping load cars—sometimes. Those and other mindless activities were not what I thought about at work though. I thought about where I was in my career, in life, in the universe. Or maybe not. The days just took care of themselves, and if I thought about anything there'd always be a clock ticking and a bell about to ring, such as a soccer match for Bertrand that evening or pick up some flour on the way home for Thetis, or it's time to schedule next year's annual vacation, but I better consult with the family first. Not mindless stuff, but mundane nonetheless. I did study customers quite a bit, both for fun and insight. I had a friend who worked in a camera store in the 1970s and '80s, a time when fine art and 35 mm photography filtered down to the masses, or at least to Everyman. George said he could almost always tell what brand of camera a customer was looking for, or could be talked into, immediately when he or she walked in the door. He worked in one of the last remaining dedicated, family-owned camera stores in the city, maybe even the country, a small shop with an unencumbered view of the front door so that he saw everybody as they entered, better than any electronic eye or facial recognition software to come. Secretaries in short skirts and cheap discount-store shoes were Minolta customers; junior executives would look at Canon automatic exposure cameras; and the art school crowd always were suckers for Nikon Fs, but maybe a used Leica M series rangefinder camera if they had long, dishwater blonde hair, pale skin, and a kind of lax stride. Every salesman would understand what George was saying, that you often can size up a customer based on his or her looks and dress. That's how psychiatrists work, too, making their diagnoses before the patient even reaches the couch the first time. I played the same game, trying to surmise what a customer might be looking for, or trying to guess just how much he or she might we willing to spend on a certain item.

I don't think any of this is what Bertrand was asking about though. What separates man from the lower animals is thinking. One would never wonder what a cow is thinking about, or a unicorn, though one might wonder just what is going on inside their heads. We humans are supposed to think about life and death, about past, present, and future, and about our relationships to others.

There were quiet times, down times, time out of time, when I did think about where I was in my life. I imagined other scenarios for me—maybe I could have become a firefighter, been one of the guys, had all the kids look up to me, not just my own son, and occasionally actually save a life. I did that once, didn't I? Had I been born a century earlier I might have run away to sea or joined the foreign legion, or just become a prospector for gold in Alaska, where I might have lived beneath the wind and ice in my own little shack with provisions I stocked every fall to get me through the winter, then I'd pan or pick for gold again come spring.

I don't know what I would have done differently, or should have, but I thought about such things at times. Mostly, though, it was one day at a time, just like for most other people. I didn't have a grand plan.

I told Bertrand that afternoon on Sugar Creek that I thought about him and Thetis a lot while at work, that I thought about what he'd be like when he grew up and who he might marry one day, and I thought about what I would tell myself when it was near the end, how I would judge myself, but that it was too early to tell just then. Then he said the most surprising thing. "Well, that's pretty much what I think about when I'm at school, thinking about you and Mom, even what kind of girl I might marry one day. And what I'll think of myself when it's all over too." Then he kept paddling for a long time without saying anything.

In his later years my father asked if I regretted not going back to college. I think we were at an Indians game and Thetis was home with the baby; Mother already had died. It was a weekday "businessman's special" at the ballpark and there weren't too many fans in attendance. We had a whole box to ourselves and we were drinking low-alcohol beer and cracking Elephant brand peanuts from a striped white-and-red paper bag and only in passing did we pay attention to the action of the field. I think the Toledo Mud Hens were the visiting team.

"Well, I'd have to wear a suit if I were a college grad," I said, but Dad told me not to be clever. Did I think not having a college degree had held me back—that was the question.

"You know you're smarter than most people who come out with a bachelor's degree," he said.

"So what would I have needed college for?" I replied.

"See, you're still being a smart ass." We both smiled.

It's not that I felt bad about working in a sporting goods store all those years. In truth, I couldn't settle into a nine-to-five job when I was younger. The sporting goods store proved to be my salvation, sort of, or at least a safe harbor. All the equipment I would see, whether golf clubs on stands or kayaks suspended from the ceiling or bicycles poised for takeoff, suggested movement and activity, life itself. Over time I learned to ask people what they were going to do with their equipment and they would tell me, usually. Hiking the Appalachian Trail. Skiing in Utah. A guided bicycle tour through Spain. Sometimes I'd remember a face or two and ask how it went: Oh, yeah, it was great. Got cut up a bit, or sunburned, or dehydrated, but it was OK. Yeah, really great. Well, thanks for asking. One customer even sent me a postcard from his travels. To: Dwight, c/o Dick's, Carmel, Indiana. It was postmarked from some town deep in the Great Smoky Mountains in East Tennessee. I showed it to Bertrand, when Bertrand was young, of course, and he immediately went to an atlas and mapped a route to get there himself.

I'd risen to floor manager in later years and had even turned down an offer to move to Pittsburgh for a job in corporate. I'd thought about it but that would have required Thetis leaving her hospital, which was where she had most of her friends. And Bertrand would have had to change schools, something that would have troubled Thetis, too, if not him so much.

Dad said that he wished he had pursued higher education. "You've greased one bearing, you've greased them all," he said. "You decommission a locomotive and it feels like a funeral, but after one hundred times you don't care."

Well, work was just something you did to earn a living and then you went on with your life—your family, planning a vacation, insulating the house for winter. It doesn't seem so bad while you're inside that bubble but when it's over and you're looking back on your life it doesn't always seem like much of an accomplishment. Except for the children, of course, whether it's one child like Thetis and I had or an entire brood. I read an article in the paper once, or maybe it was *Time* magazine, that claimed we lose our usefulness to the species at about age thirty, meaning our only purpose in life is to reproduce. Leaving aside that thirty seems like an awfully low cutoff point I understood the article well enough. We think our life has meaning and purpose but biology says there is only one purpose, which is to reproduce. Maybe that's why people still believe in God. Otherwise we're no better than a fruit fly.

Dad persisted in tweaking me about my future throughout the game that day. He said it's not too late, I could still pursue philosophy or, if the air might be too rare up there, what about law school nights?

I could have become irritated with him—"What, it's you who doesn't think I'm successful enough!"—but Dad only was looking out for me. I do question my decisions though. The proof is that I continue to think about these things.

Professor Bogdanovic, do you agree with Hegel that spirit moves through history for the purpose of revealing itself, or is it nonsense that the future can somehow determine the past?

No, philosophy was out. The law potentially could have been interesting, especially trial law. They make TV shows about trial lawyers, never patent lawyers, right? We all like someone who can best another though it often has to be disguised as the struggle for truth, justice, and the American Way, even the triumph of good over evil. It's just that when one side wins and one side loses as in a medieval joust, or a football game, we are exultant ourselves. That's what we like—winners and winning. But law was out. I had an acquaintance who studied law because he believed in the search for truth and justice. He was just a humble middle school teacher and he decided to go to law school nights—perhaps his father suggested that to him too—and he became a lawyer. "The adversarial system is the greatest feature of

our judicial system," he argued. "Each side fights as hard
as it can, which is how the truth wins out." After twenty
years, though, he said Shakespeare was right—first, kill all
the lawyers. And it wasn't because he'd misread *Henry VI*
like so many people have. It's because the lawyers really do
know too much, like a safecracker who can figure out any
combination.

I NEED to get away. I fill my time with hikes and bike rides
and volunteering but that's all it is—filling time. My existential loneliness is too cerebral; I'm beginning to feel alone
because I have no one to talk to, no one to lie beside me at
night, no one to plan getaways with. I'd ultimately declined
Bernie's offer to help in Chicago but perhaps I'd been
unfair to him. Flipping a house, or an entire neighborhood,
shouldn't be faulted out of hand. If Donald Trump can be
a real estate mogul, why not him? Some people think all
money is dirty while others just think it's the bottom feed-
ers that are dirty. It's quite unfair. Judith Prime continued to
intrigue me though. She was doing well—I knew this because
I'd visited her website several times in the weeks since I went
north. She posts a running tally of her closings, that is, the
cumulative value of all the properties she's sold to date much
like Labor Day telethons that tally pledges and contributions
in real time. That's not why I visit her site though. I don't
do porn, I'm not a trespasser, but I do like to consider her.
There's a celebrity-like quality to realtors, though I know
it's a well-crafted image, no more real than a publicity still
from a movie. Down the rabbit hole, *eh?* I like the picture
of her on her home page best, one palm up holding a big
dollar sign and the other hand on her hip, and she's wearing a red dress with a black sash, two strings of pearls over

her plunging neckline. She's a little short, a little frumpish, maybe, but so was Elizabeth Taylor. Well, she's no Elizabeth Taylor and I'm not Richard Burton. I'd just like to see her again; she was certainly comely enough that last night in Chicago, someone I could talk to, someone with her own story to share even if just across a table with subdued lighting. I wouldn't need much of a pretext to meet up with her again either. I can tell her how much I enjoyed my visit to Chicago, that I'm thinking of moving there. Maybe she can help me find a place! Or I could assist her in the real estate business. Lots of people get bored with retirement—she'll accept that.

"Dwight, how are you?" an ebullient-sounding Judith Prime says when she comes on the phone. I had called her office and the receptionist had put me on hold at first. "I'm so glad to hear from you. What's up?"

I do tell her how much I enjoyed my earlier visit, how much I learned in such a short period of time, and how small Indianapolis felt once I got back home. I tell her I've been thinking about the real estate business, how the economy is really picking up and that, while I don't need the money, it's not that I'm broke or anything, it would be nice to have enough money to go on cruises and buy a nice car, a luxury car or a Corvette, and of course I'd need a little extra income if I were ever to relocate to Chicago permanently. I'm getting excited as I tell her these things, excited that she's listening to me, and I suggest coming up in person to discuss possibilities with her directly. "I don't have a real estate license but maybe you can use a runner or something."

There's a pause at the other end of the line after I finish babbling and then Judith almost gushes into my ear. "That would be wonderful, Dwight," she says. "I'd love to speak with you. Wow, this is such a surprise but I'm so glad to hear from you. Are you still working with Bernie?"

I tell her we're still friends but that, I don't know, I was looking for something new, whatever that might be. "I mean, if I'm going to move to Chicago, or even just work there, why would I work for someone who's still in Indianapolis?"

There's another pause, then Prime says, but almost curiously, "Okay. Makes sense." She asks when am I thinking of coming up and I'm about to blurt out that I can come up right away, but I tell her next week because I know I shouldn't appear too eager. "Well, I'll book you a room in the Best Western near my office. That way you'll get a discount."

I dress warmly for my trip this time as it's getting downright cold: insulated field jacket from L.L. Bean that's not too frayed at the cuffs, wool scarf with a faux Burberry pattern I picked up on sale at Macy's, and lined lambskin gloves. I drive up in the afternoon as I'm to meet with Judith the next morning. I don't know why I'm rushing but at least I'm aware that I'm doing so. I'm not sure what I'm hoping to find but I am hopeful, which is the important thing. I haven't felt this excited in a long while.

I have time on my hands after checking into the hotel, which is near the lakefront, so I decide to go for a walk. There's a sandy beach up and down the waterfront and the sun is low in the sky behind me. I'm walking toward Evanston. The lake is calm and the sand is solidly packed; my shoes leave impressions but not deep ones, and the main thing is I don't slide back or squish as I walk. Not many people are out, but I see a couple of young lovers under a blanket and there are kids on mountain bikes trying to hack it in the sand—I think they're having a harder time than I am. I see the lights from Evanston in the distance and it's a bit of an illusion—I think the suburb is close but I'm not sure. I decide to walk all the way and I reach a small park in about thirty minutes, then I'm into the city proper in another ten. It's completely dark by now and the temperature has dropped into the low forties but that just makes the street lamps glow more vividly while the yellow-cast light behind the apartment windows is warmer and more inviting than usual, lives playing out on disparate stages.

Quite a few Northwestern University students come and go on the streets and everyone seems happy, or at least profitably occupied in one activity or another. They're all good-looking kids, clear skin, healthy, and thin; what is it Garrison Keillor always said about children in Lake Wobegon? This is not the same population one would see on a typical community college campus. I can't say I see anything wrong with anyone's behavior or demeanor, yet I'm suddenly resentful as hell. What makes these kids so special and my kid is dead. *Huh? Huh?*

I continue to walk. I'm hungry and I stop in at Lou Malnati's Pizzeria for some Chicago-style deep-dish pizza. The wait staff all look perky and robotic at the same time and everything they say is scripted, from the "How are we doing today?" greeting upon arrival to "Have a good one!" on departure. I order a small pizza with lots of cheese and wash it down with a couple of beers. It's a weeknight but the joint is jumping and the prattle and clinking of glasses ricochets off the walls. At least there's no hand-drawn smiley face on the check when the waitress comes by again.

The streets are still crowded when I've finished my meal, which surprises me, but I look at my watch and it's not late at all. Chicago's in the Central Time Zone, which partly explains my disorientation, and I manually adjust my watch.

What to do? I have Judith Prime's phone number and I decide to call her. Maybe she's still in her office. After all, business is good, isn't it?

"Sure, we can get together this evening," she says. It's not an unfriendly tone but it lacks the kind of enthusiasm I might have been hoping for. "Where are you?"

"I'm on Sheridan Road. I can catch a taxi easy."

"Well, there's nothing more for me to do in the office tonight. They have a bar at the Best Western. How about I meet you there in, say, fifteen minutes."

The hotel bar is little more than a niche along one wall of the first-floor lobby between reception and the hotel swimming pool. The bar itself is short, maybe six stools, and there are a handful of café tables scattered beyond them. Goblets and glasses hang upside down in a wire rack and several dozen bottles of whiskey are on narrow shelves in front of the mirrored back bar. I tell the bartender, a young woman, that I'd like a Grant's, neat, but they don't have Grant's so I order a Jameson Irish Whiskey.

"Neat?" she asks me, then she smiles and apologizes. "You said that already, didn't you?" She has quite a sweet, winning smile, I think, and when she serves up my drink it's a double. "On the house," she says, and she apologizes again for her earlier error, but I slip her a ten-dollar bill anyway. There is no one else at the bar or at any of the tables.

I'd arrived back at the hotel rather quickly and after several minutes of sitting alone I'm reminded why no one really wants to be a traveling salesman or woman. This place doesn't even have a jazz trio on a makeshift stage off in the corner performing the Gershwin songbook. I do wonder what kind of sales people come here though—I didn't notice any major corporations or industries nearby and there are hotels closer to the university so it's not going to be textbook sales or educational consultants.

Judith Prime soon comes in. I see her first through the revolving doors and I'm about to call out to her but catch myself. I'm the only one in the bar and she's not going to miss me. Judith waves, then crosses the tile floor. Her heels are quite loud. I stand when she reaches the table and she turns slightly, throwing her shoulders and head back, and I understand that I am to take her coat. I do, carefully folding it lengthwise, and then I fit it over the back of one of the chairs. I do not have time to pull her chair out, though; she's seated herself.

"So you've decided to make some money after all," Judith says, speaking rather breathlessly. Then she reaches for my drink and finishes it. "Order two more," she tells me.

When I come back from the bar with our drinks I see that Judith is powdering her nose. It's not common to see a woman powder her nose or face in public anymore. She's using a small, round compact. "Busy day?" I ask.

"Yes," she says without looking away from the little mirror. When she's finished she puts the compact back in her small clutch, what looks to be made of lizard skin, real or fake I can't tell, and I don't recognize the small logo sewed into one seam either. I feel Judith is very anxious this evening.

"You were working late," I say. I'm trying to be empathetic, to *appear* empathetic.

Judith consumes her fresh drink in one dump, sighs, and wets her lips with her tongue. I ask if she's put her day behind her and that brings a reluctant smile to her face.

"Did I ever tell you I'm such a bitch sometimes?" she says.

"It's a tough business you're in."

"You're sweet."

We chat a little—How's Bernie? He's doing fine; What do I think of Andrew Luck? He holds on to the ball too long; How do you stay so fit? Oh, you're making me blush, Judith.

The last question—How do I stay fit—is my opening, I think, and it's thrilling to be able to address Judith in the second person, second person familiar. "And how do you stay so lovely?" I ask. I'm so hopeful at that moment. It's like the look from across a room when you meet a woman's eyes and she doesn't turn away but tilts her head a little; it is like the touch of a hand that lingers a bit too long on yours. It's so promising.

Yet Judith looks at me quizzically. "What?" she says. It's not spoken in anger, but it's never good when a woman demands that a man explain himself. I remember that much from my better days.

"Well, I'm just so impressed with how successful you are in your career, how together you are, if you know that expression," I say. "I mean, I think you're so, well, so very vital."

Judith continues to look at me, *scrutinize* me is the word here, and then she reaches for my drink. She smiles and I wonder what she's thinking.

"Well, anyway, let me tell you what's on the agenda for tomorrow," she says. "I'm looking at a four-plus-one on Bryn Mawr Avenue that's being rehabbed. Twenty-four units plus assigned parking. You know what a four-plus-one is, right?" I don't so she tells me—four floors of apartments over parking spaces that are partly below grade. It was a common building style in Chicago in the 1970s. No one's living in the property now but a couple of units are finished—the model, and one for a caretaker. She could use someone like me to move in for a few months to make sure the contractors are doing their job and provide some security at night until the project is completed. "Free rent, of course, and we'll supply the furnishings. And you'll make a little money." Then she leans forward and tweaks my nose. "And if you're lonely at night just look for the adult services ads in the back pages of the alt press. Enjoy yourself, Dwight."

The verdict is in—I'm a fool. How could I think this woman had anything other than a professional interest in me? What clue or suggestion was there otherwise? But I've been misunderstood, I want to protest, yet I know Freud was right—sex is the subtext of everything. I'm humiliated.

"Dwight, is there a problem?" she asks. I notice that she's pulled my little glass of whiskey over to her side of the table again. She is very sexy, even coquettish—is she acting like this to punish me? Or is it to make an exclamation point— Mr. Bogdanovic, what were you thinking!

"O would some power the gift to give us to see ourselves as others see us." This always was one of my favorite Robert Burns quotes. Indeed, what seemed not real to me neverthe- less was the only reality that others could see. I'm just a sour, lonely widower, an aging rooster in the dry, dirt front yard. A cartoon Dagwood with no balls! I move my hand slowly across the table to take back my whiskey glass and I finish it, then I put the glass down softly but firmly. "I've made a mistake," I tell the woman. "I've not been honest with you but worse, I've not been honest with myself. I hope you're not too offended." As I rise to take leave—it's clear I'm not doing this four-plus-one thing, I'm not staying in Chicago— Judith smiles kindly at me. She's like a nurse or matron who is *understanding*. It almost kills me and I smile wanly at her but I do think she is not a bad person at all. Not at all.

THE REALITY is I'm alone; when Thetis died it was like the final out in the ball game. We'd arranged for hospice care for her but it was nothing like I expected. Oh, a nurse came three times a week, was on call for emergencies, and billed Medicare a fortune, I'm sure. Anything she told us we could have read on WebMD, though, and Thetis knew a lot more than she did anyway. It wasn't the nurse's fault that she worked for the medical-industrial complex and I didn't want to make her feel bad so I just smiled and nodded each time she came and went. I'd wondered where the hospice was, but Thetis said she was just glad she could remain in her own home—hospice was a concept, not a place, she said. Fellow nurses from Saint Vincent came to visit, friends from church as well. We made up a day bed in the living room because of the expansive window light there and Thetis loved the sight and sound of passing cars and dogs barking at each other or kids shouting as they ran or biked to a nearby playground. When her eyes began to fail badly she still wanted to come downstairs for the day and she'd ask me to go to the window and describe in detail what I saw—the color of a car, the breed of dog, the ages of the children, the light fading but not gone.

"Talk to me," Thetis said one day.

"About what?" I wasn't being dense or diffident. I wanted to limit my response to what she really wanted to hear.

"That time in Bloomington."

"The bicycle race?"

"You were too old to compete."

"Only students competed. I knew that."

"But you wanted to buy one of the red bicycles as a souvenir."

"Well, you liked that old movie about the race, didn't you?"

"Oh, yes. Dennis Quaid was so handsome!"

We talked about a lot of things, lots of "remember when" and "Do you think that little candle shop is still open" or "I wonder whatever happened to the Morgans, you remember, that couple we met in the state park" stuff. It felt like stumbling across old familiar songs on the radio, a very ordinary and good feeling we allowed ourselves to experience. We avoided the morbid as much as possible, not that there's any dishonor in sadness, but why feel worse than you have to? We might become wistful in the long shadows of the past but that's as close to tearful as either of us wished to be.

Caring for Thetis took quite a bit of my time, not that I wasn't dedicated to her welfare and comfort, but it was new to me. It's not the kind of experience you can prepare for. It's not nursing. It's something different, a little like caring for a child because the person is totally dependent on you, but it's not a child. I think the big difference is the "payment now due" aspect. The commitment to marriage is lifelong and entered into freely and willfully, yet everyone knows it will end one day, the "in sickness and in health" and "until death do us part" conditions of the arrangement. Now it was ending. Payment due.

I never was a good cook so I frequently brought meals home from a nearby restaurant. I didn't tell Thetis at first that I was doing this and she didn't let on that she knew, but one time she said, "Can you ask them to use less parmesan in the lasagna and maybe a different tomato sauce?" and I was just happy she could still crack a smile. But I broiled chicken and baked potatoes and steamed vegetables well enough, though over time I had to chop up all the food into very small bites for her, even wait until the food reached room temperature before serving it. I refused to make a puree out of anything or use a blender except for smoothies though.

Cleaning the bedpan and changing adult diapers was unpleasant and we didn't really speak at those times; I like to think Thetis understood I was doing what had to be done and that the only positive reinforcement I needed was her implicit trust in me. And, besides, she occasionally was strong enough to limp over to the toilet if I served as a crutch; I resisted in all cases saying something dumb like "Good girl!" but sometimes I had to stay in the bathroom with her.

"Look away," she'd say then and I'd stare at myself in the mirror over the basin and try to understand what it was I was thinking at those moments. I knew I also was getting old, waiting my turn, and who would help me on and off the can?

I bought a high wall mount for the flat-screen TV in the living room, one of those articulated models that could lift the TV higher, then allow you to turn the screen so that it angled and faced downward a bit. When a rerun of *Touched by an Angel* with Roma Downey and Della Reese came on one afternoon Thetis joked that she must be getting close, which she was, but even gallows humor was something to appreciate. I told her that I could look for the *Ghost Whisperer* with Jennifer Love Hewitt if she wanted to watch that but Thetis said I should wait until she died, then maybe she'd reappear, that is, if the program were to come back into production.

"Do you have any regrets about marrying me?" she asked me one time. I feigned incomprehension.

"You know what I mean. Did you ever think you might have been happier with another woman?"

"That's a funny thing to be asking. Really queer, you know."

"Do you love me?"

"Is it because you doubt me that you ask?"

"I just need to hear it again."

"I love you."

"Well, did you ever look at another woman?"

"Did I ever look at another woman? Did Jimmy Carter ever look at another woman?"

"He says he did."

"Well, there's your answer."

"With lust?"

"No, never with lust. Just in awe sometimes."

"Yeah, like Jennifer Love Hewitt's bosom, I bet." We both smiled then, which always was the punctuation mark to our little Neil Simon-like dialogues.

Leaving the house was difficult for Thetis and impossible near the end. The last time I was able to take her somewhere nice was several weeks before she died. We had a folding wheelchair that I employed to push her around the block when the weather was inviting and one day I decided to stuff it into the trunk of the car, put Thetis in the passenger seat, and drive to a new outdoor shopping mall, the kind that is made to look like a real cityscape with sidewalks and parking spaces right in front and individual storefronts. Shopping may seem banal but, again, the ordinary was what I was looking for. The displays, the merchandise, and the people coming and going could only be viewed as stimuli.

"There's an ice cream shop, Thetis," I said. "Would you like to go in? A furniture store? We don't need any furniture but it might be nice to see the latest styles."

I was reaching. "Or we could just go up and down the block a few times." She said she would like that best, but we did stop by a candy store. She quoted Forrest Gump, the "Life is like a box of chocolates" line. I bought the biggest box they had, but only soft-filled chocolates as they'd be easier to chew, and I said something stupid like we would have all the time we needed to finish them.

Thetis requested that she be buried next to our son at Crown Hill. I told her that we could obtain a plot at Crown Hill, but not in the military section. "You understand," I said. But if we could have obtained a plot next to Bertrand in the military section I would have wanted to be buried there too.

When the time came I decided on a private burial, the presence of a priest being my only concession to my wife's faith, and I hosted a kind of wake at the house prior to the interment. I sent word to her friends and colleagues that they could come by on a certain night between certain hours and that they should make donations to Saint Vincent or any charity of their choice, it didn't matter. No flowers either. Quite a few people came to the wake and had little stories to share.

"Did Thetis ever tell you about the flood?"

"The Biblical one?"

"Well, it was of Biblical proportions. It was the time the seventh-floor pipes burst. That was the winter of 1996, you know. It was so cold some of us stayed at the hospital all week. We just used some of the extra patient beds but we didn't have to pay $2,200 per night. They say pipes burst all over the hospital from the freezing. There weren't enough people in housekeeping to keep up with the mess. We had to close one ward altogether. Funny that Thetis wouldn't mention that. Maybe she blocked it out. I know I tried to."

What could I say to a story like that? I just took the woman's hand in mine and thanked her for coming, for being a friend.

I'd had the wake catered, mostly sliced fruits and mixed nuts and turkey meat between squares of Mary Jane white bread buns with wooden toothpicks to hold everything together, but plenty of wine choices too. It wasn't a particularly smart event and I don't know if anyone cared, or noticed. It was mostly women who came and I swear two or three were overly interested in how I was coping and whether there was anything they could do to help me in my time of need and all that.

CHAPTER 11

I try to fill my time these days with small pursuits and odd jobs. The screen in one window needs mending; rotting trim under an eave needs replacing. I can handle all that. The county needs volunteers for a voter registration drive— I guess I should consider that too. What next—a Tuesday night bowling league? Well, I have to draw the line somewhere. I continue to bicycle, of course. It's a satisfyingly solitary thing and sometimes I travel deep into the back country, anywhere there are old fire trails to follow or even along the bluffs overlooking the Ohio River, a current that never stands still. I pedal hard and if I'm tired I stop to rest, then I get back on the bike and go some more. I don't have an itinerary and I don't use GPS. If the sun is getting low in the sky and drops behind the trees I keep going. Once I was lucky enough to find a historic inn down in Brown County, the old artist colony territory, that let rooms and I was the evening's conversation piece, everyone wanting to buy me a drink or at least hot cocoa. Once I saw a highway intersection in the distance and lights from the attendant motels and restaurants and I pedaled there for the night; I know the clerks were talking about me after they gave me my room key, quietly giggling as they watched me load my bicycle upright in the elevator.

It was yet another time I just pulled off the road in the Hoosier National Forest and rolled my bike over the fallen tree trunks and through the little rivulets from a recent rain. The forest floor then was dotted with Virginia bluebells and yellow coltsfoots, little sprouts coming out of the ground as they always do in the spring before the treetops are fully leafed out, and the rotting leaves left over from the previous fall and old pieces of peeled bark added a smoky scent to the air like walking through a charred and abandoned house after a fire. Then I came across an obsolete lookout tower, one made of narrow steel girders riveted together and rickety wooden stairs leading all the way up. I leaned the bicycle against a railing, pulled down the two-by-fours that feebly blocked my passage, and let myself in. The stairs were steep but I stepped lively and pulled myself up by the rails as necessary and when I reached treetop level my chest swelled like a bellows. I wondered what it would be like to live up there, or in a lighthouse, all the world in 360 degrees and only you to watch over it. The horizon was a bit uneven from the watchtower, though, the crowns of the trees fuzzier the farther out I looked, and the wind swished in my ears while hawks glided above and smaller birds, the usual jays and robins and wrens, flitted from branch to branch. Bertrand wanted to be a park ranger, didn't he? All boys do at one time or another. Or was that me?

I also walk in the woods out by Eagle Creek Park on the west side of Indianapolis. The park features rugged trails and steep drops along the rim of a large man-made lake and you might see an occasional hawk or eagle perched on a long limb or later in the day airplane contrails that fare well against the setting sun. Or a fisherman on the pier casting bait for walleye, a dog off its leash, a Cub Scout troop on an explore, everything is normal, everything is as it always was.

I'm walking through the woods now and the boughs hang over me like a canopy, the carpet under my feet is a crunch of dry leaves and pea gravel and I come upon young lovers at the crest of one hill—she is leaning back on her forearms on a smooth boulder and he is on one elbow hovering over her. I behold the woman's knobby shoulders and mane of hair that waterfalls from the back of her head as the young man buries his face farther into her bosom—to be young again, of course.

I move on to the beachy area of the lake and I see mothers tipping their toes in the water and children splashing and paddling with their hands, and their giggles and shrill voices overwhelm the squawks of geese overhead. Cars hum as they pass by on a causeway in the distance and there is not a dark cloud in the sky, only cotton candy and laundry fluff. And as I walk along the shoreline I look out at the other side of the lake, it's maybe a mile across and a kayak cuts a "V" in the distance, an egret stands on one leg in the shallows, and I feel my head bob and roll like a buoy.

Back on the main trail I see walkers from the Indianapolis Hiking Club, they're easy to spot with their binoculars and cameras, the women in straw hats and men in cargo shorts, and I step aside to leave them pass.

"I've seen you before, haven't I?" a lady says to me. She is in the middle of the pack and I see her stop and turn to consider me, then she drifts back toward me after all the other hikers have gone around a bend. "Why don't you join us?"

I like friendly, trusting people. The woman is narrow of frame and straight as a ladder and she has short, grey hair, unprocessed and unmoussed, and her open expression suggests a lack of guile whatsoever. I smile but am not sure of what to say and so I stand silently before her.

"Are you all right?" the woman asks. I stand there, aw-shucks Gary Cooper style, and I tuck my hands into my pants pockets.

"Sure, yeah, I mean, I think so," I blabber. "You just caught me by surprise."

"Well, I see you out here a lot. Why don't you walk with us?"

I don't have an answer. All I can do is tell the woman how considerate she is, and I do think that's admirable. I could give her a reason but how can I explain that what I really want to do is cross over to the other side of the water, cross over just like the primitive people say, cross over to the other side, but not for the fool's gold of one's own immortality, it would just be a kind of symbolic victory for me; my life mattered because I did live it too.

"Some other time," I say after an awkward pause.

The woman smiles. "That's what you tell all the girls, I bet," she says.

The woman is quite appealing, I realize—slim but not frail, dressed adventurously in desert tan hiking shorts and a chambray shirt, no straw hat—and I ask for her name. "Mariah, with an *h*," she tells me and then she waits for me to respond, my turn. "Well, some other time," I say again, even more sheepishly than before, and I follow the woman with my eyes as she shrugs and turns, then lopes after her fellow hikers.

Several weeks pass and I wonder why I was so reticent with the woman in the park. I think it's because of my bad experience in Chicago, or is it because I feel guilty, disloyalty to my late wife being the charge? Still the woman had piqued my interest. What was her name? Mariah, yes, and I decide to reach out to her. *What do I have to lose?* I tell myself. *It'll be even more awkward if I bump into her again on the trail and I haven't even given her my name.* Or some such nonsense. It's a different kind of attraction this time, that's all, and it proves to be easy enough to find the woman—I simply leave my phone number with the Indianapolis Hiking Club and they promise to pass it on.

I fumbled a bit when she called a few days later—"We met last month at Eagle Creek? On the trail?"—and Mariah said that of course she remembered me, that she had been looking for me each time she'd visited the park since. It was that easy. On our first few dates—Starbucks, a visit to the art museum—we exchanged information about ourselves, as is natural. Mariah, too, had been widowed; she had a daughter and granddaughter who lived locally and a son who'd moved to New York, "the acting bug," she called it. Now Mariah and I do very standard things—a movie and dinner out, Saturday morning farmers markets, and especially bicycling on the Monon.

Mariah owned a crappy Chinese Schwinn, a cruiser model no less, something they use on the boardwalks in Atlantic City with high handlebars like a chopper motorcycle and big, round fenders like a '48 Lincoln, so late that summer we went looking for a better bike. She could have afforded a new eight-hundred dollar Trek but I brought her instead to a bicycle action project in the inner city that took in donated bikes and taught local kids to fix them, then gave some to the kids themselves and sold others to raise money for additional programs. The little shop was housed in donated space in the basement of a cathedral-like mainline church, all limestone and stained glass on the outside, a bit of faded glory on the inside. Bikes were stacked up one against the other down a hallway in the basement and other bikes were in various stages of repair on workstands in an adjacent room. A lanky, laid-back black man by the name of Billy Williams ran the show—after Williams introduced himself I asked if he was familiar with the former Chicago Cub of the same name and he said it was he in the flesh, and then he grinned broadly. "People always ask me about that other Billy," he said. "Never met him though."

They had quite a few decent bicycles for sale, mostly steel-framed Japanese models from the 1960s and '70s, and several stout Chicago Schwinn Traveler and Collegiate models, too, any color you want as long as it's yellow, red, or black. It seemed to be part of his business model that Williams would interview all new customers and he spoke to Mariah at some length—she explained that she worked for the courts in their guardian ad litem program and Williams had many questions about her duties and what happens to kids when they leave.

"I run this place to help kids myself," he said with a wave of his hand. "A lot of these kids, they come from homes that you wouldn't exactly call a home." Mariah said she felt guilty that she couldn't do more for her charges and that mostly she reported on allegations of abuse and neglect, got in the middle of custody battles, and partnered with other social service agencies when necessary.

"There usually are two new kids coming into the system for every one we push through," she lamented.

In the end I helped Mariah pick out a decent Raleigh Sprite from the 1970s, one with a lugged frame, single stem-mounted shifter for the five-speed derailleur, and a special gold metal flake paint scheme. "Let me take a picture of you on it," Williams said after we'd fitted the bike to her. He pulled out a Fuji camera that took small, instant-developing pictures like the old Polaroid Land Cameras and after he

snapped Mariah's picture we all stuck our heads in as the
camera ejected the film, then as the film developed before
our eyes.

"It's for my collection," Williams said. He pointed to a
large corkboard on a far wall I hadn't noticed before and
there were dozens and dozens of pictures pinned to it.

I ASK Mariah to accompany me to some of my weekly slow
pitch softball games. A lot of the guys bring their wives or
girlfriends, so why not me too? I was trying to be one of the
guys after all, or at least act normal. There are five teams in
our league and we play twice a week; one team always has
a bye but most of the guys usually come out and drink beer
with everyone else just the same. I play second base because
I don't have a very strong arm and I bat either second or
seventh as I'm no power hitter. We play from April well into
October.

"You should bat at least .500 in softball," Martinez says.
"Put the bat on the ball. Plant your right foot." Martinez
is short, a proverbial spark plug of a guy, and he likes to
give everyone advice. LaVerne, one of only two blacks who
start for our team, plays right center field and bats cleanup.
"Just get on base," he likes to tell people, "and I'll bring you
home." He's a slugger and often true to his word. McAuliffe,
who was a triple threat in high school, lost one leg to diabetes a couple of years ago so he coaches now. He orders the
T-shirts, makes out the lineup, and even leads the players in
the de rigueur "Go team!" shout before each game.

It's a sixty-plus league and most of the guys were jocks
in high school; they say one guy on a different team made
it to Double A minors. Some guys who excelled in baseball
when they were younger won't deign to play slow pitch but

the guys I know still like to drive the ball and they have quick reflexes and good gloves too. They're not as fast on their feet as they used to be, which I'd say is the main thing. Also a few players don't come back each spring. Sometimes it's injury but other times it's cancer or emphysema or kidney failure so we scramble to find new recruits. A few of the guys wear armor, hard plastic cups, and shin guards and the like, and of course Tommy Copper knee supports which I know is a superstition but if it makes them feel better why not. I wear a "Rip-It" wire mask at second base with my cap turned backward as there's nothing soft about a softball if it takes a bad hop and hits you in the mouth.

The venue where we play is comprised of two clay diamonds with badly rutted outfields, harsh lighting for night games, and a wooden shack for concessions. Some younger teams compete there as well but we're the best customers because we remember the park when it wasn't so bad—it was never good—while the more competitive and better-funded teams all have moved to the suburbs. The park is third-generation family-owned, not taxpayer-supported like all the nicer parks, and I guess we old guys won't let it die. Yes, there we were playing a child's game, but I always remember what a fellow player named Spider once said in the dugout: "Gentlemen, just think of all the people our age who can't get out of bed and here we are, still able to swing a bat and run the bases," and I knew he was right. It was a call for gratitude if not grace itself.

I remember the first time I took Mariah to the park: a handful of women had come out that evening, the usual wives and girlfriends, a couple of adult daughters, and they all sat together on aluminum stands behind the backstop. It was a mild evening shading into cool and most of the players wore long-sleeve T-shirts and full-length baseball pants, the stretchy kind with narrow blue or red stripes down the sides, and the women cheered our good plays or cried, "Stop the madness," if we'd made a few too many errors.

"It's mine, it's mine," I had to shout on one play, a high pop-up to short right field. Running with your back to the infield and making the catch is never easy but I snagged the ball cleanly. I usually warm up for games by running along the outside fencing and then doing the usual stretching and bending exercises but it's the sudden stop-and-start action of the actual game that leads to a lot of soreness the next morning anyway.

I was in a good mood as I'd gone three-for-four, including a double, all clean hits, and had made only one error in six chances. We lost the game but I hadn't lost face, which is the main thing for a lot of the players, including me. After the game I suggested stopping at the liquor store on the way home to buy some sherry, which I knew Mariah liked, and I found it exciting to leave my girl, as it were, waiting for me in my Mustang as I strode inside.

Back at my place I fixed us both drinks while Mariah went upstairs and slipped into one of my robes. We'd been sleeping together for a couple of months, which I guess was inevitable. I hadn't been looking for sex and, in fact, we didn't have sex often, more just to prove we could still do it rather than a throbbing desire as if we had to have it, for either of us, I think. Mariah used the term emotional intimacy to describe our relationship but I would have settled for "comfortable."

It was only natural that Mariah would want to know more about Bertrand; I'd told her he had died a soldier, but that's about all. I'd never believed in speeches, neither mine or anyone else's, but how could I deny Mariah, let her into my home but not into my life? I knew it was unfair. I showed her an album of photos and she noted how handsome he was. The medals too—Bertrand had received a few medals and decorations in his career and I'd kept them, which might sound like an odd thing to credit but I knew from USO that some bereaved parents would refuse to answer the door when uniformed soldiers came to notify them of a death in person—two uniformed soldiers park a car with government-issue license plates in front of your house and it can only mean one thing—or they'd just toss any medals and decorations in the trash with anger surpassing despair. Or pawn them like so many souvenirs from long forgotten campaigns, fare for the real hounds of war, other people who only know how to lick the blood from someone else's wounds. But I didn't want to talk much about Bertrand's actual career in the military, I said.

WE HAVE an appreciation dinner for all the USO volunteers each January and I invited Mariah to accompany me to the most recent one. People typically attend with their spouses and I'd felt self-conscious previously, sitting at big, round banquet tables with several couples and I was the only single person there. Everyone would be friendly and welcoming, the usual questions being about how long have you volunteered and especially if you were in the service yourself. "My son was," I would say and my sympathetic interlocutors would ask follow-up questions but when they saw how difficult it was for me to answer, when they looked more closely into my eyes and saw the hurt still pooling there, they'd go back to conversing among themselves. I'd felt the odd man out. Having Mariah accompany me this time made me feel more like I belonged, or more like I was normal, though I had to quickly correct another lady at our table when she assumed

Mariah was my wife. The dinners were held at a large south side church as that's the part of town where most veterans come from, where most of the current police and firefighters in Indianapolis still live. It's not a working-class area per se and it's not that most of the cars and trucks you see in the parking lots are of an American make. It's just that it's still the 1950s there.

There were annoying albeit innocuous aspects to the dinners as there are to all catered affairs and recognition events, I suppose. The USO state leadership had to be introduced, then somebody from the governor's office, then somebody from the airport authority that had donated space to us, then acknowledgments of several big corporate donors. There's always a raffle too. The Colts donated an autographed game ball for the most recent dinner and the Pacers contributed four tickets. A local electronics store had donated a forty-inch flat-screen TV, which was the grand prize. There was innovation this year though. "Would the Gold Star parents please stand," they asked.

Would the Gold Star parents please stand? Those are the men and women who'd lost a son or daughter. There never was any bluster about war or caricatures of the enemy or "the other" or petty partisan politicking—it was a recognition of loss and sacrifice that knows no distinctions. The room was silent after the call to stand, then slowly you heard chairs pushed back, a deep breath taken, and then one, two people stood, then ten and eleven and twelve, some grim-faced, others teary-eyed, some grasping hands of spouses or lovers nearby but in the end they stood like sturdy trees that had survived a storm. Yet I was not one of them and Mariah nudged me; she nudged me twice and I was sure everyone at our table looked at us. "You have to stand," she said firmly. "You're not the only one." I scanned the room and beheld the other Gold Star parents and I knew she was right. I was not the only one to suffer and so I laid the palms of my hands on the table and pushed myself away and stood with all of them.

LATER THAT evening I decided to unlock myself and yield to Mariah everything she had wanted to know about Bertrand, what had made him a wonderful boy and what he'd accomplished but also what he'd become, a gunman, a night stalker, a transcendent figure who superintended without guilt. Oh, I'd heard rumors about how he died, I told her—an effort to kill a Taliban chief that had gone very wrong when a local agent betrayed the mission; a helicopter crash one furtive, moonless night in Pakistan that our Defense Department couldn't acknowledge; even the one about coming home to kill a deserter from his previous unit, then he'd been killed in a shootout with MPs, even that one, all rumors, I said—but the government would only say he was KIA, *killed in action,* the bare outline of a dagger by his name in all the official documents. I opened up that rainy evening while we were seated at the kitchen table in my house, each of us nursing a cup of coffee that went cold in time as I just kept talking, revealing so much, wanting to see if she could take it but wanting to know if I could let go too. I had a story I was holding inside me, yet by holding so much in I was denying Bertrand his rightful place in history; by holding it in I simply was compounding his death.

"His last letter home, he wrote about what he might do after he got out of the service," I told her. "Maybe go to college and study political science, but only at a good school. Or start his own security firm; guys he knew talked about that. 'All the bankers these days want private security and bulletproof glass in their limos,' he wrote. 'They pay really well in New York, even better in London, I hear.' Or he might buy a ranch in Montana and raise llamas. 'I don't get a chance to spend much money. I salt most of it away. Can I give you the account number just in case?' Or maybe he'd stay in, help train the next bunch, as he termed it. 'What do you think, Pops?' That was the last line in his last letter, other than the closing, 'Love you both, Bertrand.' I'd caught the wariness in his words, not so much the sarcasm as the wry, wizened way of an old hand at this, whatever this was that he was doing. Sure, I wanted to know more about his life in the military but I don't think I was living through him. He was his own man. I was proud that I'd raised him right, and I won't judge him now, and I have to believe the other soldiers did what they had to do too.

I hand her the stack of Bertrand's old letters that I'd kept, all bound in twine and neatly knotted, and I watch as she pulls the little bow tie loose at either end; the letters fan out like a deck of cards on the table.

"Which shall I read?" she asks.

"I know them all by heart," I reply incongruously.

Mariah picks an envelope that's shiny like gift wrap and colored like mocha. Bertrand had purchased the envelope and paper at an outdoor market in Jalalabad. I watch as she reads it in silence; I notice every time she winces, each time her head kicks back a little, but also the inflation in her cheeks when she might be trying to stifle a smile and I want to tell her it's all right to laugh because Bertrand could be really funny at times, even in the worst of times, but I say nothing. It was the letter about payments Bertrand had had to make to a local warlord who'd keep the Taliban at bay, but he wasn't so sure. He'd also described the heavily cloaked women who sold bakery goods from woven grass baskets in the markets and all the old CB radios in shelf-worn boxes and misprinted soccer jerseys stacked high on old folding card tables and the cheap, made-in-China frying pans and kitchenware for sale.

"Did you get to the part about the Captain America comic books?" I ask. "He told me later that he wanted to pose with the guy who was selling all the superhero comics from a cardboard box, just squatting in the dirt with a bunch of dog-eared American comics, but he thought better of it, leave no trace and all that. What kind of war zone is that, right?"

How can anyone understand anyone else's pain? But I was wrong to think like that. Two million years of human evolution doesn't mean we are all different; it means we are alike. The philosophers' questions—*How can we know the thing in itself? How can I know anything outside of my own perceptions?*—are all shattered by Darwin. My pain is not unique and it is not inscrutable.

I look at Mariah, this new woman in my life, decent and potent as Thetis was, and I reach with my hand to take hers, I hope she understands that she doesn't have to say anything, and as I take her hand it is like kidskin and so we go forth hand-in-hand up the stairs to bed like the pilgrims we all are, life is for the living, it's really no choice at all.